A Brewtiful Kind of Love

Tia Marlee

A Novel Choice Press

Contents

To My Sister and Brother-in-Law
It's not easy to step into a ready-made family, but C, you did it with such grace and ease.
The life you are building together with the sweet babies you are raising is a testament to your compassion, commitment, and love.
I'm blessed to be a part of your journey.

Chapter One

Ashlan

AIR BRAKES SQUEAL OUTSIDE, then a long streak of yellow rumbles past the window, and I almost cry. Almost. "Ezra, come on. You've missed the bus now." I sigh, my shoulders sagging like a deflated balloon. He's been dragging his feet all morning.

"Almost ready, Mom," his little voice calls from down the hallway.

You'd think he'd be excited to be in kindergarten and out of the house. I'm grateful for Mom watching him while I worked, but that meant he spent a lot of time with adults and not enough with kids his own age. Kindergarten is good for him. At least that's what I tell myself every day when I drop him off.

"Here," Mom says, breezing into the room, her plush robe tied tight around her middle, and slippers still on her feet. She's apparently in no rush this morning, unlike me . . .

"Don't forget his lunch." She passes me a small lunch bag decorated with sea animals—Ezra's latest obsession.

I loop the handles over my arm and slide my feet into my coffee-stained sneakers. "Thanks. Tell me this gets easier." I lean down to adjust the laces and hear her gasp. I shake my head. *What now?*

Slowly, I turn around, my eyes closed against the ridiculousness that I'm sure awaits me. Ezra has been dressing himself for school, and it's been . . . interesting. I open one eye first and immediately wish I hadn't. "Ezra, what are you wearing?" My voice rises an octave, disbelief coloring my tone.

He shrugs his little shoulders and looks down at his clothes. "Mrs. Morgan told me we were learning about the ocean this week." He takes his backpack off the hook and shoves his little arms through the straps.

I stand there, mouth gaping like a fish out of water. "Did she ask you to dress up?" I ask, desperately searching my memory for a flier that mentioned coming to school in a costume.

"Nope," he says, shaking his head. "I just wanna." His expression leaves no room for argument. Once Ezra decides something, it's impossible to change his mind. Certainly not in the thirty seconds I have to get him out the door before we are both incredibly late.

Mom stifles a giggle, and I glare at her. "It's cold out today, why don't we . . ." I start, but he cuts me off.

"I know. That's why I'm wearing these." He sticks out one leg and points to the gray thermal pants. "They're to keep me warm."

Mom snorts before she leans down and gives him a hug and a peck on the top of his head. "You have a great day, Ezra." She walks into her bedroom shaking her head and murmuring something about him being just like me.

"Okay," I say, trying to figure out how to get him into something that more closely resembles school clothes than an ineffective scuba suit. "Can we leave the snorkel set at home at least?"

He shakes his head. "Nuh uh, how will I breathe in the water? Mrs. Morgan said we were gonna see some ocean animals, and I want to be ready."

That explains the camera he has dangling around his neck. The old cuckoo clock on the wall lets out the first call of the hour. I'm out of time. Looks like I'll be dropping Scuba Steve off at school. At least he's wearing swim shoes and not flippers. Though the rash guard, swim trunks, thermals, and winter coat are not my favorite ensemble, I decide he'll be warm enough, anyway. *Pick your battles.*

Ezra chatters about all the things he hopes to see in the ocean today, and I bite back a sigh. He's so literal sometimes, and no amount of arguing will change his little mind. Occasionally, I pull the "because I said so" card, but more often than not, I let him roll with it. What's it hurt?

Once I get my little explorer settled in the booster seat, and get on the road, I can finally think. I glance in the rearview mirror and drink him in. It's not been easy being a single mom, but I wouldn't trade him for the world. When I found out I was pregnant, I sat in the bathroom and cried. His dad had scoffed and told me it was my problem. That there was no way Ezra was his, and I wasn't ruining his life by holding him back with some kid. I roll my eyes at the memory. I guess love really makes you blind. How else could I possibly have been with someone so heartless and self-centered?

The school drop-off line is in sight, pulling me to the present. "Here we are," I say, flipping on my blinker and pulling into the line. "I hope you have fun and learn lots of things."

Mrs. Reese, the other teacher in Ezra's class, steps up and opens the door. Her eyes bulge out when she takes in his outfit. "Good morning, Ezra," she says, laughter in her voice. "I see you're ready for some ocean explorations today."

He nods his little head as he slides down from the car seat. "I hope I get to pet a shark!" he says. "Bye, Mom." He grabs his backpack and joins the other kids by the school wall.

"Don't forget your lunch," Mrs. Reese calls, holding it out for him to take. "Have a good day, Mom." She winks and closes the door.

I take one last look at my little boy in his imaginative wardrobe and head to work.

🐟 🐟 🐟 🐟 🐟

The doorbell chimes as I step inside the Coffee Loft. The familiar scent of freshly ground coffee instantly soothes my frayed nerves.

"Morning," I say to Aurora as I slide behind her and stuff my bag under the counter. "Sorry I'm a few minutes late. Ezra missed the bus."

"No problem," she says. "You're right on time. I need to pop to the back and take a phone call. The regional franchise manager requested a meeting this morning." She raises her mug to her lips and takes a big drink. "Decaf just doesn't pack the same punch." She sighs and grabs an apple turnover from the pastry display.

"Only a few more months to go," I remind her.

She rubs her swollen belly. "Thank goodness," she mutters as she walks away.

I watch her disappear behind the swinging door to the back and smile. Aurora and Bradley have had a whirlwind romance. Last year at this time, I was watching her avoid him like the plague. Now, they're married and having a baby.

I shake my head and get busy wiping down the empty tables before the next rush of customers. When the door chimes again, I look up to greet the newcomer and drop my towel onto the floor. "Aiden!"

He opens his arms and I'm in them in a heartbeat. "Hey, sis. Surprise!" He squeezes me tight, and the smell of his laundry soap mixed with his cologne makes me sneeze. "Bless you."

"What are you doing here?" I ask, stepping back and looking him over. His usual attire of a navy blue suit, white button-up and tie, have been replaced with a pair of well-worn jeans, a red flannel shirt, and a pair of work boots. "Planning to cut down some trees?"

He smiles. "Something like that, but first I need some caffeine." He points to the menu board. "I hear the Coffee Loft is the best coffee in town."

I chuckle. "Don't let Ms. Daisy hear you say that." Beats and Eats has been a staple in Piney Brook for as long as I can remember. The all-day diner has the best sweet tea around, but the coffee . . . I shudder. Let's just say it leaves something to be desired.

"Never." He winks at me and goes back to looking at the menu. "How about two Lofty Americanos, and throw in a half dozen assorted muffins?" He pulls his wallet out and passes over two twenty-dollar bills. "Keep the change."

I put the money in the till and stuff the change in the tip jar. "Why two?" I ask, as I fill a box with muffins.

"One for Beau."

He leans casually against the counter watching me, and I have to hope he misses the way my breath hitches when I hear his best friend's name. "Beau's in town, too?" I go for nonchalant, but apparently miss the mark because Aiden is scowling.

"He's my best friend, Ash. He's off limits." Aiden waves his finger in the air.

I set the muffins on the counter and turn to make the coffees. "I didn't say I was interested. Jeez. Besides, you know I haven't dated since . . ." I can't bring myself to say his name. Anyone who could abandon his son and pretend like he never existed isn't worth the breath.

"Sorry," Aiden says, clearly chastised. "I don't mean you shouldn't date, just not my best friend."

I force a laugh. "How long are you in town?" I ask, hoping to change the subject to safer territory and away from the fact that I've had a crush on Beau Travers since the first time I laid eyes on him at the age of ten.

"Well, that's to be seen. Beau's just bought a cabin up on the mountain, and I told him I'd come help him settle in. I can work remotely now as long as there is internet, and this way I'm close to you guys for the holidays." He takes a sip of the coffee I just handed him and smiles. "Man, this *is* good."

I nod. "It really is the best coffee in town." The door chimes as the book club ladies file in one by one. "I've got to get to work, but call me later and we'll talk."

I watch as Aiden carefully pushes through the door and onto the sidewalk. Beau Travers bought a cabin on the mountain? Does that mean he plans to stick around?

I take my time helping each of the book club women with their orders and resetting the display of pastries, all the while remembering how Beau played with Ezra when he was home for his parents' funeral. I'd stopped by to drop off a meal, and we talked for hours while Ezra toddled around and got into anything he could reach. It was like time stood still. We'd connected then, and I almost got my hopes up that there could be something more for us one day.

After that, I always wondered if he'd ever move back to town, but as months turned to years, I figured he had put down roots someplace else.

So, what's he doing here now? And how long does he plan to stay?

Chapter Two

Beau

THE RUMBLE OF A truck engine filters through the tree line, and I set aside the ax I've been swinging for the last twenty minutes. I toss the leather-palmed gloves I purchased at the hardware store in Barberville alongside the ax. My hands ache, so I rub my palms together, grimacing as I apply pressure to the sore spots. Rough calluses line the top of my palm, making me glad I'd at least thought to grab the gloves when I was stocking up on renovation supplies. Luke, from Barberville Hardware, hadn't taken advantage of the city slicker after all.

"What have you done?" Aiden, my best friend, asks, stepping down from the cab of his truck.

I motion toward the splintered logs scattered around us, each one a testament to my rusty skills. "Well, it looks like I've chopped some wood." The scent of fresh pine fills the air, and I breathe it in. This is why I wanted to come home. There's a peace in these woods that

I could never find in the city. And after the last few years, peace is exactly what I need.

"You could have just bought firewood, you know," he says, gesturing to the pile of split wood. "Unless you're channeling your inner lumberjack." He stares me down. "Seriously, bro. Are you having a mental breakdown?"

I roll my eyes. "Just because I *could* buy it doesn't mean I want to. I came out here to get away from the hustle. Get back to my roots." I tilt my head up toward the sunshine and grin. "Feels good to do something with my hands."

Aiden snorts. "From the looks of this place, your hands are gonna 'feel good' for a long time, then."

I turn and try to see the cabin through his eyes. The front porch sags on the right side, the paint's chipped or peeling off most of the outer walls, and the roof has definitely seen better days. "It's a work in progress," I mutter. "Besides, you're looking at the wrong things." I point to a spot behind his head where the sun is shining through the tall pines. "That's why I bought this cabin."

"And you didn't just pay to have it remodeled before you moved in because . . ."

"Because that's not nearly as satisfying as doing it myself. Haven't you ever wanted to get your hands dirty?"

Aiden looks down at his perfectly manicured nails and shakes his head. "Not since I was about twelve." He shudders. "To each his own, I suppose. Tell me there's wifi. I took the rest of this week off, but I'm on the hook for work again come Monday." He reaches in the truck and pulls out a bag and two cups of coffee. "Here, I figured you could use this."

My worn hands slip around the warm cup, and I bite back a groan. It wouldn't be in my best interests to let on just how much work we have ahead of us. "They're coming in the morning to set it up." I leave out the part where they said it would take a miracle to get the internet signal strong enough to be anything but adequate out here. That's a problem for tomorrow.

He must sense there's more, because he raises a brow and pins me with his deep green eyes. The same shade as the ones I used to see in my dreams. Ashlan Dewitt, my best friend's very off-limits little sister.

"What aren't you telling me?" he asks.

"That you're a pain in my rear," I joke.

"Hardy har har." He slings an overnight bag over his shoulder and closes his truck door. "Why don't you show me where I'll be staying in this cozy little nightmare in the woods?"

I bump into him with my shoulder. "Right this way, your majesty." Aiden snorts and rolls his eyes but follows me up the rickety steps to the worn porch. "Careful, a few of the boards need to be replaced."

Crack. I turn in time to see Aiden's foot go through the broken floorboard. Lunging forward, I drop my coffee and reach to grab him just in time to keep him from falling. His coffee falls, joining mine on the porch, the contents running down the broken boards and seeping into his pant legs. Thankfully, the bag of muffins landed just outside of the wet mess.

"Thanks for the warning," he deadpans, pulling his leg free.

"Are you good?" I ask.

He stands, carefully placing his feet so as not to step on another weak board. "Yeah, I'll live, but this porch is project number one. Someone's going to break a leg."

I nod. "The wood's right there," I say, pointing to a pile off the side of the porch. "We can start on that as soon as we put your stuff inside."

Aiden grabs the empty cups and pastry bag and carefully makes his way across the porch. Once he's made it through the front door without falling through the porch again, he sighs in relief. I nearly chuckle at his dramatics, but I suppose I'd feel the same way if my foot had just gone through the floor.

"What in the world?" Aiden moves in a slow circle around the living area. "When was this thing built? The 1800s?"

"It's got good bones," I reply. "The cabin is old, but it's structurally sound. Besides, I kind of like the exposed-wood look."

Aiden snorts. "There's a difference between exposed wood and straight up logs. This place looks like an old man was playing a game of real-life Lincoln Logs." He drops the bag and empty cups onto the kitchen counter.

"My favorite toy growing up," I joke. "Seriously though, with some sanding and stain, this is going to look great."

Aiden's eyebrows rise behind his hairline. "Yeah, great. I'm beginning to think you came up here to live like a hermit all alone. It'll be tough to find a woman who shares your . . . vision."

I shake my head. "I'm not looking to settle down." Besides, the one woman I've always wanted, I can't have. Everyone I've dated since leaving Piney Brook I've compared to her and, surprise, no one measured up. No one captured my attention quite like Ashlan.

Especially after spending time with her two years ago when I was back home.

"This is going to be more work than you let on." Aiden sighs. "Can I see my room now?"

I lead him down the short hallway off the main living area. "The bathroom is here," I say, swinging open the first door on the left. "Your room is right next to the bathroom. Mine is at the end of the hallway, and this room," I say, opening the only remaining door, "is going to be a guest room."

Aiden steps inside the room that will be his for the time being and shuts the door. "I'll be out in a minute," he calls.

Satisfied that he's settling in, I head back to the kitchen to toss the coffee cups in the garbage and wipe down the sticky counter. Once that's cleaned up, I open the bag and inhale the scent of sugary goodness. I pull out a blueberry muffin and grab a plate. This is going to be tasty.

When Aiden joins me at the counter, he reaches for a muffin, carefully peeling back the wrapper and splitting it into halves before taking a huge bite. "So," he says, chewing his muffin. "The porch."

I pop the last of my muffin into my mouth and nod. "Yep," I say once I've swallowed the bite. "I'm ready when you are."

While Aiden finishes his food, we talk about the weather, work, and my plans now that I'm technically jobless. All the while, I'm trying to figure out how to bring up his sister. How can I ask about her without making him suspicious?

"And Mom said, and I quote, 'You both better be here for family dinner on Sunday,'" Aiden says, dusting the crumbs from his fingers as we make our way outside to the broken porch. "So, looks like we have dinner plans this weekend."

Family dinner. At his mom's. Where Ashlan lives. I can do that.

"Sounds good," I say, trying to keep my face impassive. The last time I saw Ashlan was at my parents' funeral two years ago. She was a warm, soothing beam of sunlight during the fog of my grief. She made it seem natural to talk about what I was feeling, unlike anyone else. And we talked about other things, too. And laughed, even. I didn't want to assume anything, though. They say you're not supposed to make big life decisions while you're grieving, so I didn't scoop her up and take her with me when I went back home. Even if I'd really wanted to.

Since then, I've forced myself to stay away. I've had a crush on her since I was seventeen and she was fifteen, but Aiden would have lost it if he'd suspected. So, I buried my feelings. I figured it was a childhood crush, and it would go away on its own once I was away at college. I was wrong. Every time we came home to visit, I found myself making excuses to stay up late playing games or watching movies with her.

I considered just telling Aiden how I felt once she graduated high school, but then Aiden mentioned she was dating some guy named TJ. He was happy for her until one day, during our Junior year of college, when he came in fuming about her being pregnant and TJ claiming it wasn't his. Aiden was irate, claiming he would maim anyone who came near her again. I tucked away the idea of telling him I liked her and tried to forget about it.

I was doing a pretty good job, too. Until the funeral. Seeing her with a toddler on her hip had done something to my heart. She was so beautiful and confident in how she cared for her son. It made me crave things I had no business wanting.

Like a family of my own.

With her.

"How do we repair a porch, anyway?" Aiden asks, bringing my attention back to the moment.

"Carefully," I deadpan. "Come on. We need to rip up the rest of these boards."

"Show me the way, Bob Vila." When I don't laugh, he continues. "From that show, *This Old House*, or something."

I nod. "Yeah, my dad loved that show." I hand him a pry bar and a pair of gloves. "Let's do this."

"Sorry," Aiden says, slipping the gloves on and kneeling down near the corner. He wedges the pry bar under a loose beam and gives it a tug. The wood breaks free with a groan, and sends him falling backwards onto his rear. "This porch is trying to kill me," he says, pushing to stand and rubbing his backside.

"Nah, you're doing just fine on your own." I laugh when he shoots me a dirty look. Having my accident-prone best friend here to help is going to be fun.

Chapter Three

Ashlan

"Can you set the table, please?" Mom asks, handing me a stack of plates.

"Of course," I say, "but you handed me too many." I go to put two plates back in the cabinet, but she stops me.

"No, your brother and Beau are coming for dinner. I'm sure I told you that." She turns and pulls open the oven door to check her rolls.

My hands shake as I put the two plates back on the stack. "No, pretty sure you left that part out." Beau is coming for dinner?

"Oh, well. You know now," Mom says.

I take the plates to the table and set them down. "What time will they be here?" I ask, looking down at my worn t-shirt and baggy lounge pants. If I'd known we were having company, I'd have done something with my hair other than a messy mom bun.

The front door opens just as mom answers me. "Oh, here they are. Right on time."

"Uncle Aiden," Ezra calls, running full speed into my brother. Aiden swings him into the air before holding him on his hip and giving him a high five. "Hey, little man, how've you been?"

Ezra beams. "Good. Who's that?" he asks, pointing at Beau.

My breath catches as he steps around my brother and into full view. His dark hair's a little longer and messier than I remember, and he's grown a beard. It suits him. He looks like a man who lives on a mountain—rugged, strong, handsome. His deep brown eyes remind me of melted chocolate. I could dip strawberries into them and . . . wait. No, that's weird. I shake myself out of my stupor and plaster a smile on my face. "Nice to see you, Beau."

He nods in my direction. "Hello, Ashlan. Thanks for having me, Mrs. Dewitt."

"Oh, Beau, you're like family. You don't need an invitation to join us for dinner. Isn't that right, Ashlan?" Mom turns and stares at me, a twinkle in her eye.

Oh no, what is she up to? "Uh, of course," I squeak out.

Aiden locks eyes with me and mouths "off limits." Like I don't already know that. I've been crushing on the guy since I was a kid. Clearly, I knew a lost cause when I saw one. What would someone like Beau Travers want with a broke single mom who still lives with her mother? Nothing, that's what.

"Here, let me help," Beau says, picking up the stack of plates and placing one at each seat.

"I'll do the forks," Ezra yells, wiggling to be let down. Aiden lowers him to the floor, then steps back and watches him take off to the kitchen drawer.

"No running with forks," I call.

"Yes, Mom." Ezra counts out five forks and holds them carefully in his hands as he tiptoes toward the table.

"You can walk faster than that," Mom says, shaking her head.

"Nuh uh, I'm a sloth. And sloths walk ssslllloooooowwwww," he says, drawing out the word.

Aiden snorts. "I seem to remember a time when your mom loved to pretend to be animals, too. Except she liked to pretend she was a cheetah and scratch me."

I huff. "I only scratched you when you were trying to take my toys."

Mom laughs. "You two certainly kept me on my toes." She grabs a bowl of spaghetti and passes it to Aiden. "Take this to the table, dear."

By the time sloth Ezra has placed the forks down by the plates, the adults have placed all the food on the table.

"Mom, can we pray now? I'm hungry," Ezra asks, scooting himself into his booster seat at the table.

"Yep," I say, hoping that the sloth part of the evening is over, otherwise, the food will be cold before we get to eat.

We all bow our heads as Ezra starts the prayer. "Dear God, thank you for the animals and food. Oh, and Uncle Aiden and Mommy. Amen. Wait, also for candy. Amen."

I hear Beau chuckle and sneak a glance in his direction. He's smiling and it lights up his face. Could he be any more handsome?

"Right, Mommy?" Ezra asks.

I look at my brother for help. He's too busy smirking at me to throw me a bone. "Uh, can you repeat that?" I ask.

"I said, sloths have their babies upside down in a tree. 'Member? We learned that at the zoo." He takes a bite of spaghetti, the red sauce smearing his little cheeks.

"Oh, yeah. That's true." I twist my fork in the pasta and bring it to my mouth.

"Did you give birth to me upside down?" he asks.

Aiden snorts, clearly enjoying this time with his nephew. "No, I wasn't upside down," I answer after I finish chewing my food.

Ezra nods. "That's probably good. Otherwise, I could have bonked my head." He scoops up more spaghetti and takes another bite.

Thankfully, I'm saved from any more uncomfortable questions when the conversation turns to Beau and his new cabin. Aiden recounts falling through the porch and then falling on his bum when they were trying to repair it. "It's a death trap, I tell ya."

"It's not that bad," Beau says, playfully jabbing Aiden on the arm. "It's going to be amazing when it's finished."

Aiden rubs his arm. "Yeah, if it gets finished. There's a ton of work to do."

Beau sighs. "That's half the fun," he says, taking a big bite of pasta.

"I'm sure it's going to be perfect when you're done," I say.

He looks up and meets my eyes. "Thanks, Ash." Neither of us looks away, and I can feel heat creeping up my neck, staining it red. "Ouch!" Beau says, whipping his head towards my brother. "What was that for?"

"No making goo-goo eyes at my sister, man. It's weird."

I swear I see a bit of pink at the top of Beau's cheeks where his beard doesn't cover. Is he blushing?

"I wasn't making goo-goo eyes," Beau mutters. "Whatever those are."

Mom laughs. "Aiden, Beau and Ashlan are both grown adults. If he wants to make eyes at her, he's allowed to. They get to make their own choices about who they find attractive."

"What's 'tractive' mean?" asks Ezra, clearly absorbed in the adult conversation.

"It's when two grown-ups like each other and want to get to know each other better," Mom answers.

Ezra looks from me to Beau and grins. "So, you think my mommy is a tractor?"

Beau chokes on his food. Aiden jumps up from his seat and slaps him on the back, and I slide down into my seat. Could this be any more awkward?

After Beau stops choking, Aiden answers Ezra. "No, because he's my best friend."

Mom scoffs. "All the better, I say."

"Mom," I squeak. "Can we not?"

"Why not?" she asks. "You've had a crush on Beau for as long as I can remember. You're both adults. He's moving back to town. I don't see what the problem is."

Aiden sputters. "The problem is, he's my best friend. He thinks of her like a sister. Right, Beau?"

All eyes are on Beau as he squirms uncomfortably in his seat. "I think we should change the subject."

Aiden drops into his chair, his mouth hanging wide open. Mom claps her hands and smiles like she just won the blue ribbon at the state fair. Ezra giggles, unaware of the mess that's being made around him, and I . . . I can't take my eyes off of Beau. Could he really see me as more than Aiden's little sister?

"She's not your sister," Ezra says, clearly confused by the turn in the conversation.

"No, she's not," Beau says, looking down at his plate and pushing the spaghetti around.

Aiden shakes his head. "I can't believe this." He takes his plate to the kitchen and places it on the counter. "Thanks for the invite mom, but Beau and I have to head back now."

"But you didn't even finish eating," Mom protests.

"Yeah, we did," Aiden says, taking Beau's plate from the table and putting it in the kitchen. "I'll see ya later, kid," he says, ruffling Ezra's hair. "Bye."

He practically drags Beau from the house. As the door clicks shut behind them, Mom sighs. "That went well, don't you think?"

I push my chair back and lift Ezra down from his seat. "Let's go, dude, it's bath time."

"Ash?" Mom says. "You okay?"

I shake my head. "Not now." Ezra slips his little hand in mine, and we make our way down the hallway to the bathroom, leaving our plates on the table. I'll clean it up after Ezra's in bed. Right now, I need some space.

We step into the bathroom, and I start the water for his bath. "Bubbles tonight?"

"Yes, please." Ezra undresses and slides into the warm water. I put the bubble soap into the bath, and he swishes it around, giggling when he gets bubbles on his chin.

He plays in the bath for a bit before I wet his hair and soap him up.

"Mommy," Ezra says, his eyes squeezed shut to keep the soap out. "Do you think I'll ever have a daddy?"

My heart sinks. "I don't know," I breathe. "Sometimes it's only mommies and kids. Sometimes that's better, don't you think?" I reach down and tickle his sides.

He giggles and squirms away. "Yeah, okay."

I finish rinsing the soap from his hair and body and help him out of the tub. Grabbing his favorite fluffy towel, I wrap him up and give him a hug. "I love you, Ezra."

"Love you, too, Mommy." He steps back and dries himself off.

"I'll grab your pajamas and be right back." Stepping out of the bathroom into the hallway, I take a deep breath. I knew he'd ask about having a father one day, but I didn't expect it to be so soon. It's a good thing TJ left town for college right after he found out I was pregnant, or I'd drive over to his house and kick him right in the shin.

"Here," Mom says, stepping out of Ezra's room and passing me a stack of clothes. "I figured you'd need these." She leans in and envelopes me in a hug. "I'm sorry I pushed tonight. I just don't want you to forget that you deserve love, too. And I think Beau would be perfect for you." She steps back, squeezes my arms one more time, and then slips into her room and closes the door.

"Mom," Ezra calls. "My butt's getting cold."

Laughing, I shake my head. This kid of mine. He's the only love I need.

Chapter Four

Beau

AIDEN IS QUIET THE entire ride back up the mountain. His silence is making me sweat. When we pull into the driveway, he turns the engine off and stares out the window. "How long have you liked my sister?" he asks.

"I . . . what?" One innocent comment and now I'm facing down my angry best friend.

"You heard me," he says, turning to face me. "How long have you liked my sister?"

I debate lying, but Aiden's my best friend. "Since we were seniors."

He gasps. "Since HIGH SCHOOL?" he shouts. "Are you serious?"

"I never acted on it because I knew you'd be upset." I hold up my hands. "I swear. I have no intentions of pursuing your sister."

Aiden's face turns furious. "And just why not?" He pushes open his truck door and jumps down. "Now she's not good enough for you or something?" He's yelling and shoving his shirt sleeves up as he stomps over to my side of the truck.

I scramble to get out of the cab and onto solid ground. "What? I never said that." I'm getting whiplash here. First, he's adamant that I can't be attracted to his sister. Now he's mad that I'm saying I'll stay away?

"I see. So, she was good enough for you to like in high school, but now that she's a single mom, you don't want her?" Aiden vibrates with anger.

"Listen, man. I'm not sure what your deal is here. It doesn't matter to me if Ashlan has six kids. She's beautiful, funny and kind . . . everything I could ever want in a partner. I don't plan to pursue her because she's your sister."

"Good," Aiden says. "Stay away from her. She doesn't need someone else coming in and messing up their lives." He stomps into the house and slams the door.

So much for his blessing.

I head inside and grab a glass of water before heading into my room and closing the door. Aiden hasn't packed his stuff and left yet. That has to be a good sign, right?

As much as I like Ashlan, I couldn't risk losing Aiden. He's been more than my best friend all these years. He's like my brother, and the only family I have left.

Slipping into my pajama pants, I climb into bed and pull a pillow over my face. My thoughts go right to a certain beauty and her adorable little boy. Aiden's reaction tells me all I need to know. He'll never be okay with me dating his sister. I roll onto my side and vow to let her go.

*   *   *   *   *

The fire alarm startles me from my sleep. I take a deep breath and inhale the pungent aroma of burnt toast. "Aiden?" I call, jumping out of bed and running down the short hallway.

"Nothing to worry about," Aiden says, waving a dish towel by the smoke detector. "Just burned my breakfast."

I rush to the window and yank, but it doesn't budge. I move to the next one, and it gives way with a groan. Frigid air blasts inside, making me shiver. In all the commotion, I'd skipped putting on a shirt. I open the back door to create a cross breeze, and the alarm finally stops blaring. "Dude, seriously?"

Aiden shrugs. "Sorry, you don't have a toaster. I had to use the oven. I was trying to get the wifi to work so I can log into work, and forgot about the toast." He tosses the burnt toast in the trash. "Now I have no breakfast and no wifi. Happy Monday to me," he grumbles.

I can't help it—I burst out laughing.

"I'm glad you find this funny. I guess I'll go to Mom's and work from there today. Maybe she'll feed me breakfast." He closes his laptop and puts it in his work bag. "I'll be back later."

He's talking to me this morning. I had wondered if he'd give me the silent treatment. I run my hands over my face in an effort to wake myself up. "See you," I call as he walks out the front door without responding.

Okay, then. I glance at the time on the stove display. May as well get this day started. First things first, coffee.

I pull the old Keurig machine out, pop in a dark roast pod, and press start. Except, nothing happens. *Seriously?* After trying everything, including another electrical socket, I finally admit defeat.

Guess I'll be heading into town for a cup of coffee . . . and a new pot. I can't put in the hours here un-caffeinated—that will never work. Back in my bedroom, I pull on a well-worn pair of jeans and a thermal shirt. Without sparing a glance in the mirror, I slip my feet into my boots and grab the keys off the hook.

The truck starts up, and I pull down the long driveway to the road that leads to town. It's a good thing the heater warms up fast, otherwise I'd be a popsicle by the time I reached the main strip.

I hate going into town. I moved up the mountain to be away from the hustle and bustle of people. After college, Aiden and I went to Austin to make our mark on the world. The traffic, fake dates, and constant activity were an enormous change from home. I'd thought big city life would be exciting and fun all the time. Turns out it was a nightmare. But Austin was the new tech center of the US, and if we were launching our own startup, it's where we needed to be.

In the end, I developed horrible anxiety, and by the time we sold the company, I was working almost exclusively from home.

Aiden loved it and constantly tried dragging me on dates to get me out of the house. It made sense that he'd choose to stay in Austin now.

I'm nearly to the Walmart when I see a sign for the Coffee Loft. I pull my truck into the only open spot and put it in park. May as well start with some coffee, and that cup Aiden brought me was pretty good. It has absolutely nothing to do with a certain brunette who may be working inside. Nope. Nothing at all.

The door chimes when I step inside, and my heart sinks just a little when I don't see Ashlan behind the counter. Though, the smell of freshly ground beans and the promise of caffeine has me perking up.

"Welcome to the Coffee Loft, how can I help you?" the barista asks—Aurora, according to the name embroidered on her apron.

"Just a hot coffee, as big as you've got, with cream and sugar, please." I glance at the baked goods in the display case beside me and my mouth waters. "Throw in a blueberry muffin if you don't mind."

"One lofty hot with a muffin. You've got it!"

"Hey, do you . . ." Ashlan says as she pushes through the swinging door from the back of the cafe, her words dropping off as she notices me at the counter. A faint blush stains her cheeks and I fight to keep a straight face.

"What was that?" Aurora asks, setting my order in front of me.

Ashlan clears her throat. "Um, I was asking if you had a minute. Someone from corporate called while I was in the office working on the schedule. Something about a mixup with the orders. She's on the phone now and wants to talk to you."

"Can you finish ringing out this customer?" Aurora asks while I watch the exchange. This would never happen in a coffee shop in Austin. Employees forgo talking to each other, or making small talk with the customers. It takes too long and customers would riot. Well, not really, but they'd complain. Loudly. I shudder. That's another thing I don't miss about living in a bigger city. Everyone is always in such a hurry. Give me a slower pace any day.

"Sure thing," Ashlan says, biting back a smile as she turns and gives me her attention. "How are you this morning?" she asks as

Aurora hustles through the door to where I'm assuming the office is located.

"I've been better." I pass her my credit card.

"Is Aiden giving you a hard time?" she asks, swiping it and handing it back. Her green eyes meet mine, and I want to drown in their depths. I give myself a hard mental shake. *She's off limits, stupid.*

"Trying to burn my house down with his cooking," I grumble.

She laughs, and a smile tugs at the corner of my lips. She's beautiful always, but when she laughs . . . it's like the heavens open up and shine right here on earth.

"That sounds about right," she says. "I hope your day gets better."

It already has, but I don't share that part. "Thanks," I say instead.

Aiden's words ring through my head, and his hurt expression flashes through my mind. I can't betray him, and she deserves someone who can give her the world. I just hope by the time she finds him, I can be happy for her.

Waving, I hustle out the door and back into my truck before I can do something stupid, like ask her out. No matter how much I'd like to.

Chapter Five

Ashlan

I WATCH AS BEAU leaves the Coffee Loft in a hurry. That conversation was about as awkward as when Billy Schmidt picked me up for prom and handed me a corsage that was clearly made for someone else. The orangey red roses clashed terribly with my deep purple dress. He spent the evening staring at Natasha Lanksford and didn't even ask me to dance once.

Clearly, last night's dinner conversation had made things weird between Beau and me.

"Thanks for handling that," Aurora says, stepping out from the back. "I guess the Coffee Loft in Bentonville got our order and called it in. Thankfully, the corporate office was able to confirm the mix up and our delivery will be here in a few hours."

"That's good. We're about out of creamer."

"I'm going to go work on payroll for a bit. Come get me if you need me." Aurora slips through the door into the back.

An hour later, I'm wiping the counters when Aurora comes out and sees the tables empty. "It looks like we are going to be slow today. You want to take off early and finish your Christmas shopping?"

I glance at the clock. "It's really early. Are you sure?"

She nods. "Yeah, I'll be okay. Ember's scheduled to come in at two and with the shipment being delayed, she'll be here in time to help stock."

I untie my apron. "If you're sure, I could definitely use the time to finish up. Ezra's really into ocean animals right now, and I'd planned to go to the mall over in Rogers to see what I can find."

"This is perfect, then. You can go do that while he's in school." She winks and rubs her hand over her belly. "I can't wait to spoil this little one next Christmas."

I smile and tuck my apron under the counter. "That baby will be so blessed. Between Bradley's building skills and your taste, you'll probably come up with some amazing gifts."

She grins. "Did I tell you he and Heath are working on the crib? I tried to talk him into buying one, but he's determined to make it instead." She places both hands over her heart. "I swear, he's like one of those romance novel boyfriends, you know."

I sigh. "If he knows anyone else . . . send them my way, would ya?" I say jokingly as the door chimes.

"Send who your way?"

Heat floods my cheeks. Of course, my brother would choose just this moment to barge in.

"She's looking for a boyfriend," Aurora says, winking at me. "Know anyone who might fit the bill?"

I'm sure I'm on fire now. My face feels so hot. "I am not," I mutter. "I was just saying her husband's too good to be true."

Aiden looks back and forth between us, his eyebrows drawn together. "I thought you liked Beau?"

"Ohhh," Aurora says, fanning her face. "Who's Beau? Why haven't I heard about him?"

I can't believe this is my life. "Beau is Aiden's best friend. You haven't heard about him, because there's nothing to hear."

Aiden nods. "That's exactly right. Off limits."

I shake my head. "You're crazy."

"I am not. I told Beau the same thing last night. Off limits. I can't have my best friend dating my sister. It's weird. He's known you since you were a kid."

"He was a kid, too," I snap. Seriously? Two minutes. I just needed two more minutes and I could have missed this entire exchange.

"Juicy," Aurora says. "If this were a book, the two of you would start dating secretly behind your brother's back.

"You better not!" Aiden says, glaring at me.

"You'll be happy to hear Beau was in here this morning and barely said two words to me. Obviously he's not interested in a small-town single mom."

"Good, at least he listens." Aiden crosses his arms over his chest, making him look like Ezra right before he throws an epic tantrum.

"I was just leaving. Aiden, I hope you have a great day. Don't burn anyone's house down, and for the love of all that is sacred, please drop this whole Beau thing."

"Fine," he says, leaning a hip against the counter. "And where are you going?"

"I gave her the rest of the day off to finish her shopping. I think she was planning to head to the mall." Aurora chimes in, ever so helpful. Thankfully, a small line of customers has formed during this madness and she leaves to handle them. I snag my purse from under the counter and wave goodbye.

Aiden follows me to the door. "Are you looking for a boyfriend, Ash?"

I push through the door, and Aiden stays right on my heels. "Weren't you going to get some coffee or something?"

"Nah, I was coming to see if you wanted to grab an early lunch."

I shake my head. "If I'm going to make it to the mall and back before it's time to get Ezra from school, I need to leave now." I press the unlock button and open the driver's door. "I'll see you around, I'm sure."

Aiden walks to the passenger side of my car, opens the door, and climbs in.

"What are you doing?" I ask. "Besides getting on my nerves."

He laughs. "I'm going with you. I don't have any more meetings today, and I need to finish shopping, myself. Plus, the mall has a food court. We can get lunch there."

"Sure," I say, sliding into my seat and closing the door. "I guess we're going to the mall."

He settles back into the seat and grins. "Sounds good to me. It'll give us a chance to catch up."

"There's nothing to catch up on," I mutter as I pull away from the curb and head towards the interstate. Should be a great afternoon.

Aiden spends the drive talking about the new company he's working for since he and Beau sold their start-up. Apparently, the video game industry is in flux right now. Who knew?

We make it to the mall and, by some miracle, find a parking space close to the toy store.

"What are we looking for?" Aiden asks, opening the door and letting me inside first.

This place is a zoo. Displays of toys overflow into the aisles, little kids are running around knocking things off of the shelves, and Christmas music blares from hidden speakers. "I was hoping it wouldn't be busy," I mutter, grabbing a cart and following Aiden through the madhouse that is Toys and More. "Hopefully they'll have something ocean related Ezra will like. He's all about animals these days, but especially sharks and whales."

Aiden nods. "Mom told me about the interesting outfit from last week." He chuckles. "That kid is definitely yours."

I laugh. "You're not wrong about that." The tension from the Coffee Loft has dissipated, and now that we're here, I'm grateful for his company. We take our time wandering the aisles and chatting until we find the ocean toys. Aiden's going crazy, putting everything in the cart, when a snide voice behind me calls my name.

"Ashlan Dewitt, what are you doing here?"

My spine tingles with anxiety, and my hands grip the cart tight enough for my fingers to turn white.

"Shopping for your grandson," Aiden says, his voice thick with venom. "The one you refuse to acknowledge."

"Why, I never!" Elaine gasps. "That child could be anyone's."

Aiden scoffs. "You and I both know the only one sleeping around in that relationship was your son."

"Aiden," I mumble. "It's not worth it."

He ignores me and steps closer to Elaine. "It's sad, really. You're missing out on knowing the best little boy I've ever met, and one day, you'll regret the way you've treated my sister."

She lifts her nose into the air and harrumphs. "I doubt that. Besides, TJ and his wife are bringing my real grandson to visit soon."

Aiden looks like he's about to burst a blood vessel. I reach out and grab his arm, giving it a squeeze before he loses it and says something he'll really regret. I wouldn't want this miserable woman to be Ezra's grandma anyway, but the rejection still stings.

"Come on," Aiden says, dropping a huge stuffed whale into the cart. "We have better things to do."

I nod and follow as he pulls the cart down the aisle and away from Elaine.

"Thanks," I say once we're finally far enough away from her I can breathe again.

"For what?" Aiden asks.

"Standing up for me." I wipe a tear away from my cheek. "It shouldn't matter, but . . ."

He pulls me in for a hug. "I know. I just hope you know not every guy is TJ. There are some good men out there who would love an opportunity to love you and Ezra."

I give him a watery smile. "Maybe, but they aren't in Piney Brook."

He bumps my shoulder with his. "You never know."

By the time we get back home and unload all the bags into the house, it's time to pick Ezra up from school. "I'll go," Mom says, grabbing her keys. "You two stay here and get that hidden." She shakes her head. "I don't know where It's all going to go."

Aiden laughs. "I'm sure there's room somewhere. Besides, a kid only gets so many Christmases to get every toy their hearts desire."

"You're going to spoil him," I say, looking at the mountain of things Aiden purchased.

"Good! He deserves to be spoiled!"

"I'll be back with him in twenty minutes. Hurry and get that stuff hidden. And *you're* helping wrap all this," she says, pointing to Aiden.

He laughs as she walks out the door.

"Seriously," I say, looking around. "I don't know where we can hide this much stuff."

Aiden shrugs and scoops up a couple of bags again. "Let's go. You can take me up to the cabin and we can store it there."

I shake my head. "Just take your truck." I can't go to Beau's cabin unannounced.

"It's in the shop. Brant said it would be ready in the morning."

I roll my eyes. "What's wrong with the truck?"

"Nothing," he says. "Just needs new brake pads and tires, and Brant had to order them."

"So you walked over here?"

He nods. "Where else was I going to go?"

I shake my head. "How did you plan to get home?"

He grins at me and makes a stupid finger shooting motion. "I figured my favorite sister would take me."

Of course. "Fine," I say, grabbing several bags. "But you're driving."

After loading up the car, I call Mom and let her know the plan while Aiden drives us up the mountain to Beau's cabin.

"Home sweet home," Aiden says sarcastically when he pulls into the driveway.

The cabin sits in the middle of a clearing surrounded by beautiful old pine trees. The sun streams through the trees, brightening the yard. It's older, but it has a ton of charm. "I like the new porch," I tease.

"Ha ha," Aiden says, putting the car in park and turning it off. "By the time he's done, most everything will be new. I still don't understand why he didn't just hire someone to come out and fix it up."

We both get out of the car and head around to the trunk. While he opens the trunk and starts grabbing bags, I glance back at the cabin and smile. It looks aged, in a good way. Like it's lived a lifetime of stories already and is waiting for its new chapter. "All it needs is a bit of a facelift," I say.

He shakes his head and side-eyes me. "Careful, you're starting to sound just like Beau."

I blush, but shake my head. "You just can't see the beauty in it yet."

"That's what I said," Beau says from behind me, making me jump and hit my head on the corner of the trunk lid.

"Ouch!"

"Shoot! I'm sorry. Are you okay?" he asks, reaching out and feeling my head.

Tingles erupt on my scalp, running down my spine, and out to my fingers and toes. Clearly, I hit my head hard enough to do nerve damage because there's no way Beau's touch affects me like this.

"I'm fine," I say, rubbing the lump I can feel forming on my head.

"Come on," he says, wrapping an arm around me and guiding me up the stairs and into the cabin. "Let's get some ice on that."

"Sure," I hear Aiden call. "I can bring all this in myself."

"Good!" Beau calls back. He leads me to a stool at the bar and pulls it out so I can climb up. "Sit here." He turns and heads to a refrigerator that looks like it might be from the 1970s, and pulls open the freezer door. When he turns back around, he's got an ice pack in his hand. He grabs a towel from the counter and wraps it around the ice pack before placing it gently on my head. "Here. This should help."

"She's fine," Aiden says, pushing through the doorway and setting the bags down. "I could use some help, though."

Beau turns and spots the bags littering the living room. "What's all this?"

"Aiden bought the toy store today," I say. "He thought we could store it here in his room."

Beau grunts. "I see."

Oh, no. He's upset. I should have insisted Aiden call and check with him. "It's okay. I'm sure we can find a place for it at Mom's."

"No, we can't," Aiden says. "Besides, Mom did say we have to wrap it all. Wouldn't that be easier to do here?"

I laugh. "We? No sir, she said you."

Aiden sticks out his bottom lip and pouts. "Come on, sis. You know I can't wrap presents. I'd stuff everything into a gift bag."

I glance at Beau who's watching the exchange with a slight smile on his face. Maybe wrapping presents here wouldn't be so bad after all. Especially if I get to see Beau in his element.

Chapter Six

Beau

AIDEN BRINGS MORE BAGS inside, and I shake my head. Ashlan wasn't kidding. He really did buy out the toy store from the looks of it. "Did you leave anything for Santa to get him?"

Aiden smirks. "This is from Santa. Well, except the giant blue whale and the Hot Wheels track. I can't show up empty-handed, now can I?"

Ashlan slips off the bar stool and onto her feet, taking a moment to steady herself before walking over and grabbing some of the bags. "Where to?" she asks Aiden.

"Here," I tell her, taking the bags from her hands. "We've got it." When my hands brush hers, I feel the hairs on my arms stand on end. It's like brushing one of those static electricity toys they had at the science museum when I was a kid. My eyes meet hers, and I can tell she felt it too.

"Thanks," she says, her voice breathy.

"You're welcome." I finish collecting the bags and follow Aiden down the hallway, stopping at the guest room. "We can put them in here. I won't be working in this room before Christmas, anyway."

"Thanks man," Aiden says, stepping inside the room and unloading his arms. "I appreciate it."

"Not a problem." Well, not really, anyway. I don't mind the presents being stored here, but they are planning to wrap them here, too. The more time I spend around Ashlan, the harder it is to remember why I can't just ask her out like I want to.

"Aiden," Ashlan calls. "Am I driving you back to town? I need to get home and help Ezra with his homework."

"They give kindergarteners homework now?" I ask, walking back into the living room. When I was in school, we definitely didn't have homework so young.

"Yep. Mostly math and reading stuff." She sighs. "Sometimes it goes fast, and sometimes not so much. It depends on how focused he is."

"I'm good, sis," Aiden says. "I'll have Beau bring me to Brant's in the morning to grab my truck."

I inwardly groan. "That's fine with me," I lie. I'd rather stay here and work on the cabin. Away from tempting little sisters who light me up like the town Christmas tree when we touch.

"Great," she says, standing and heading to the door. "I'll see you tomorrow, then. Today was Ezra's last day of school before the break, so I took some vacation. I can come by and wrap presents tomorrow if that's okay. I'm sure it's going to take forever with the mountain of things you bought."

Tomorrow? While Aiden works? I don't think that's a good idea. "Sure, I'll help." What? That was not what I meant to say.

"No, you won't," Aiden says, scowling. "I can wrap the presents myself."

"But you just said you couldn't," Ashlan says, shaking her head.

"I changed my mind."

"You're being a baby," Ashlan says. "I'll be here tomorrow to wrap presents. If you want to help, you're welcome to take the day off and join me."

Aiden frowns. "I can't. I have meetings all day."

"It's okay. I can help you out," I say to her again. Clearly, I've lost my mind, *and* my sense of self-preservation if the look Aiden is giving me means anything.

Ashlan's face lights up. "That would be amazing, thank you!"

Aiden looks between the two of us, and shakes his head. He clearly thinks this is a bad idea, too.

"No problem."

"Here," Aiden says, opening the door. "I'll walk you to your car."

Once they are both out the door, I head out the back door to collect more firewood for the night. The temperature is supposed to drop as a cold front moves through. They're even discussing the possibility of a white Christmas. I stack the logs on the back porch where we can reach them easily, and head back inside. No central heating makes keeping the wood stove burning all night imperative.

Aiden's in the living room when I come back inside. "Thanks for letting us take over the guest room with stuff, but she's still off limits."

"No problem," I say, taking a seat on the old sofa. "I'm aware. Any reason you went crazy in the store?"

Aiden shudders. "Well, I wanted to make sure Ezra has a great Christmas, so I had planned to buy a few things."

I scoff. "That's more than a few, my friend."

He laughs. "I know. It's just . . . we ran into Elaine Price, and I watched all the color drain from Ashlan's face. That woman is the wicked witch of Arkansas. I'm sure of it. The way she spoke to Ash and about her had me seeing red. I ended up putting more things in the cart to distract us both and ended up with all that."

My heart races and my hands clench in anger. "Elaine Price?" I ask, wondering who would dare talk to Ashlan like that. She's the sweetest woman I've ever known.

"TJ's mom." Aiden shrugs. "That apple didn't seem to fall too far from the tree."

I shake my head. "I don't get it."

"Neither do I," Aiden says, standing. "What are we working on tonight?"

Thankful for the change of subject, I stand and point to the cans of stain stacked in the corner. "I spent the day sanding and cleaning the walls. Figured we could put on a coat of stain."

Aiden nods. "Let me go change and we can get to work."

🐾 🐾 🐾 🐾 🐾

The next morning, Aiden knocks on my door, waking me up. "Ready to go? I need to get into town and get to work."

I groan and crack my eyes open. The sky is barely lit. "How are you awake this early?" We were up until after midnight staining the walls in the living area.

"I set an alarm," he deadpans. "Seriously, you should try it."

I laugh. "No thanks, I am not on anyone else's schedule out here. I'll be out in a sec." I slip on a pair of jeans and pull a hoodie over my head. Satisfied I'll be warm enough, I grab socks and head to the living room. Aiden's waiting at the door, a cup of coffee in his hands.

"I see you found the new coffee pot."

He holds the cup out and nods. "Yep."

"Didn't happen to make me a cup, did you?" I slip the socks over my feet and step into my boots.

"I didn't pour it, but there's some left in the pot if you want a cup."

I nod and quickly pour myself a travel mug of coffee while Aiden impatiently taps his foot by the door. "Let's go," I say, grabbing my keys and heading for the door.

Aiden steps out onto the porch and slips on the icy steps. I watch as he works to keep himself upright, his feet sliding back and forth like he's on some exercise machine. He drops his bag and sends the mug full of coffee flying through the air as he pinwheels his arms through the air. For a second, I think he's going to catch himself, but his left foot slips too far and down he goes, toppling down the stairs, and landing on his side on the ground.

"You could have tried to save me," he says, pushing to standing and brushing himself off.

"So we could both go down?" I ask, laughing. "Besides, I thought you had it there for a second."

He looks at me like I have two heads. "Which second was that? The one where I looked like a flailing cartoon character, or the one where I landed on my face?"

I'm laughing too hard now to answer him, so I just shrug. "Need to change?" I ask.

"No way. I'm not attempting those stairs again."

Still chuckling, I turn and lock the door before carefully grabbing his bag and the railing and making my way down the slippery steps.

"Not fair," Aiden complains.

"It's not my fault you didn't grab the railing." I hand him his bag and set his empty mug on the stairs so I can grab it when I get back.

"I'll get some salt from the store while I'm out and we can salt the steps." Besides, I don't want Ashlan slipping and falling when she comes by. Though, the icy patches should be gone by then. Once the sun comes up, they'll melt off pretty quickly.

"That's a good idea," Aiden says, rubbing his hip. "I'm pretty sure I'm going to have a bruise."

"I bet."

The ride into town is quiet. I pull into Brant's Automotive and park next to Aiden's truck. "Don't forget the salt," he says. "And remember what I said about Ashlan."

I just laugh as he closes the door and I pull away. I'm almost to the hardware store when my phone rings. The number is local, but I don't recognize it. "Hello?"

"Hey, Beau. I hope you don't mind—Mom gave me your number." Ashlan's sweet voice rings through the cab of my truck.

"Hi, Ash. What's up?" Knowing she has my number is doing funny things to my insides.

"I was just wondering when would be a good time to come over. Ezra's going to A Child's Place today to play with Matti, so I have some time to myself."

I glance at the clock on my dash. "I'm running in to the store right now, so give me about an hour and I'll be home."

"Great! I can bring all the supplies. I appreciate it."

"Happy to help," I tell her, and I'm surprised when I realize I mean it. I hate wrapping presents. I'm not great at it. My mom used to wrap each gift perfectly, adding ribbons and bows. I'm lucky I can get the wrapping paper to cover the whole thing.

"See you soon," she says before disconnecting the call.

Hopefully Ashlan's not disappointed with my wrapping skills.

An hour later, I'm back home, the stairs are clear of ice, and I'm anxiously awaiting Ashlan's arrival. I grabbed some snack stuff and drinks while I was out this morning. I don't want to be a bad host, after all. Aiden may want me to steer clear of her romantically, but I'm sure he'd want me to feed her.

When I hear her car door shut, I put down the sandpaper I was using to sand the walls in my bedroom, and pad down the hall to the front door.

"Hey," I say, opening the door a few seconds after she knocks. "Need help getting anything from the car?"

She smiles up at me, and my heart skips a beat. She looks stunning today in a red sweater, leggings with Santa faces on them, and furry boots. Her brown hair is down, and it curls softly around her shoulders. I swallow, my mouth suddenly dry. Keeping my distance may be harder than I thought.

"That would be great," she says, stepping through the open door and setting the wrapping paper she was holding down. "There's just a few more things in the back seat."

"I'll get them," I say. "I set up a table in the guest room so we don't have to sit on the floor and wrap."

"Oh, that's smart!" She grabs the paper and nods toward the hallway. "If you tell me which room, I'll get things organized."

I lead her down the hallway and show her the room we'll be working in. "Here we are."

"Oh," she says, looking around. "This room is a great size, and I love the exposed wood! It feels homey."

I grin. "Aiden thinks it feels like a cave."

She laughs. "Aiden has no vision. This room, the whole cabin actually, is great. I can't wait to see it when you're finished renovating." She blushes. "I mean. I'm sure it will be beautiful."

All I can think about is her in my home when it's finished. "You'll have to come check it out, then. Maybe I'll have you over for dinner." Mentally, I slap myself. What am I doing?

Her blush deepens. "That . . . would be fun."

"I'm going to go get the rest of the things from the car." And get my head on straight. Ashlan may want to see the house when it's done, but that doesn't mean anything. It can't.

I find myself wondering if she could see herself living out in the woods away from close neighbors and the bustle of town. Ashlan deserves the world, and that's definitely not a piece of secluded land on a mountain. Though, to be fair, it's just a thirty-minute drive into Piney Brook. "Stop," I mutter to myself. She's off limits, but I'm having a hard time remembering that right now. It feels so right to have her in my space.

I gather the rest of the bags from her back seat and shut the car door. Taking a deep breath, I head back inside. I'll just keep reminding myself that she's Aiden's off-limits sister—that should help. Yeah, right.

"Thanks," Ashlan says, meeting me at the front door and grabbing some of the load. "You don't have to help me if you'd rather be working on the cabin."

She's giving me an out. I should take it. "No, I could use a break." Clearly, I'm not into doing things I should these days.

"Great!" Her eyes light up and she grins at me before spinning on her socked feet and walking down the hallway, taking a piece of my heart with her.

Chapter Seven

Ashlan

I HURRY DOWN THE hallway to the guest room, taking deep breaths to calm my racing heart. Beau Travers is going to help me wrap Christmas presents for my son. Hopefully, I don't say anything stupid. Like, Would you like to take me out sometime? Or, Have you ever considered dating a single mom? Nope. I need to keep those inside thoughts *well* inside.

"Here," Beau says, passing me the rest of the stuff he got from my car. "I think I should warn you I'm not great at wrapping."

I laugh. "That's okay. You'll get the hang of it."

I take a moment to organize all the supplies on the table. Piles of presents line the wall under a big window that streams light into the room. "We can do it one pile at a time. I figured that would be easiest, and it'll let us switch up the wrapping paper so it's not all the same." I point to two small piles off to the side. "Those are from myself and Aiden, so we'll do those last."

He nods and collects the things from a pile, moving them closer to the table. "Which paper are we starting with?"

I take a moment to decide which paper will be the Santa rolls and which will be the family paper. "Here," I say, moving the family ones off to the side. "You pick."

Beau grabs the paper with snowmen on it and smiles. "This one first."

"Do you mind if I play some Christmas music while we work?" I ask, holding up my phone.

"Nope, go for it," he says, his face drawn in and a frown tugging at the corners of his lips.

I open my music app and hit play on the Christmas playlist I've started. We fall into comfortable silence while we wrap. I finish the first present, and use the scissors to create curly ribbons before setting the present back on the floor.

I turn around and have to bite my lip to stifle a laugh. It looks like Beau is about to wage war against the wrapping paper. The man who is planning to renovate this entire cabin is losing a battle to a roll of festive snowman paper.

"How is this even possible?" he grumbles, the scissors clutched in one hand while the other tries—and fails—to fold the paper neatly around the box. Instead of crisp edges, there are crumpled corners and an outrageous amount of tape holding everything together.

"Need some help?" I ask, trying to contain my laughter and failing.

"I've got it," he says, his jaw set in determination. The tape dispenser slides across the table and hits the floor with a clatter. "Why is this so hard? It's paper and tape!"

I cover my laughter with a cough. Or try to.

He turns, one eyebrow raised, and a strip of tape stuck to his forearm. "You think this is funny?"

"Maybe a little," I say, stepping closer. "Can I help, now?"

"I've got it," he says, putting the last piece of tape in place. He slaps a bow on the corner and grins. "See," he says, holding it up.

The bow falls off the package and lands at his feet. He bursts out laughing. "Okay, maybe I could use a lesson or two."

He unwraps the mess and we start again. I take my time walking him through it, and by the time we finish, he's holding up a present even Santa's elves would be proud of. "I did it!"

I laugh. "You did. You just needed a tip or two."

He grins and grabs the next present. I'm not sure the last time I saw Beau so carefree. It had to be back in highschool before he and Aiden left for college. They were always doing silly stuff and getting in trouble together.

A few hours later, I look around the room. Only the two piles of family presents left. "Thanks for your help," I say, standing and stretching my back. "I wouldn't have gotten nearly as much done without you."

He stands and smiles. "Thanks for teaching me how to wrap presents."

I bump my shoulder into his arm. "Anytime."

"Do you have time for a bite to eat?" he asks. "I bought snacks, but we were so focused that I forgot."

We'd spent the last few hours talking and laughing while we wrapped. It was like we transported back two years and the time we spent together after his parents passed and Aiden had gone back to Austin. That ember of hope I'd felt then was burning brighter than ever.

"I need to go pick up Ezra. Maybe another time," I say, sliding my boots back on my feet and grabbing my purse.

"How about tomorrow night?" Beau asks, the tips of his ears turning pink.

Did I hear him right? "Tomorrow night?" I ask, confused.

He clears his throat. "We could grab dinner. Only if you want to." He looks away and starts picking up the wrapping paper pieces that litter the table.

"Like a date?" I ask, my heart racing faster than the last winner of the Kentucky Derby.

"Yeah," he says, turning and meeting my eyes. "Like a date. You can bring Ezra if you'd like."

Beau Travers just asked me out and included my son. Butterflies erupt in my stomach and I feel slightly lightheaded.

"It's okay if you don't," he says, turning away.

"Are you sure about this?" I ask, thinking of how Aiden's going to respond when he finds out.

Beau tilts his head to the side and studies me. "Yeah, I think I am."

"Then I'd love to," I say. "Though I think I'll see if Mom can watch Ezra this time."

He spins back around, a huge smile on his face. "I'll pick you up at six? Does that work?"

I nod my head and swallow hard. "That works perfectly."

"I'll walk you out," he says, dropping the paper he collected back onto the table. Placing his hand at the small of my back, he guides me out the front door and to my car. He opens my door and waits for me to climb inside and start it up. "I'll see you tomorrow."

"See you tomorrow," I say, grinning.

He closes my car door and steps back, watching as I pull out of the driveway and turn onto the road that leads down the mountain.

I have a date with Beau Travers.

᠄ ᠄ ᠄ ᠄ ᠄

"Good morning, Mommy," Ezra whispers as he climbs into my bed. "Grandma says it's time to get up."

I lift the covers, and he climbs down inside. "Just a minute. Mommy wants some Ezra cuddles first."

He giggles and scoots closer to my side. "Okay."

After a minute, he wiggles and rolls over to face me. "Mommy," he says, pulling up an eyelid. "Is it time to get up now?"

I chuckle. "I guess so."

"Yay!" He climbs out of the bed and runs out of the room. "Mommy's getting up now," he shouts.

I rub my hands over my face and sigh. I'd hoped to sleep in on my days off, but apparently that's not happening. Climbing out of bed, I wrap myself in my robe and slip my feet into the warm slippers Ezra got me for Christmas last year. Yawning, I pad down the hallway and into the kitchen. "Please tell me there's coffee?"

Mom smiles and slides a mug my way. "Here you are, sleepy head."

"Thanks." I take a seat at the kitchen table and inhale the rich aroma of freshly brewed coffee. How people start their day without it is beyond me.

"So," Mom says, taking a seat next to me. "How was wrapping presents yesterday?"

She was out with her friends until after I'd gone to bed, so we hadn't had a chance to catch up yet. "It was good," I say, taking a sip of the hot liquid sunshine. "We got a lot done."

I can feel her eyes on me. Heat fills my cheeks, and I can't help the smile that slowly spreads on my face.

"Did you two talk much?" Mom asks.

I nod. "Some."

"You're killing me," she finally says, throwing her hands up.

I laugh. "Actually, I was wondering if you could watch Ezra for me tonight?"

Her eyebrows shoot up so high they get lost in her bangs. "You have plans?"

I nod again. "Yeah, it seems I have a date tonight."

Mom squeals and claps her hands. "Of course I can watch Ezra."

"Watch me what?" Ezra asks, joining us at the table.

"Grandma's going to watch you while I go to dinner with a friend tonight."

Mom snorts. "I'd say he's looking to be more than friends."

"Mom!" I nod toward Ezra. "Too soon."

Ezra giggles. "Are you going on a date?"

My head snaps in his direction. "What do you know about dates?" I ask. I've certainly not been on one since I had him. How could he know what that means?

"I know that grown-ups who are 'tracted to each other go on dates and get married." He bobs his head up and down. "So, are you going on a date with Beau? He's 'tracted to you, right, Grandma?"

Mom chuckles. "I believe you're right, Ezra."

"So?" he asks, looking at me expectantly.

"How would you feel if I was going on a date with Beau?" I've had a crush on him for years, and I know he's a good man, but if Ezra's not on board, this stops now. His is the only opinion that matters. Aiden can kick rocks.

He shrugs his little shoulders. "How long until you get married?" he asks.

Mom chokes on her coffee, spitting a bit of it across the table. I stand and pat her back. "This is your fault," I whisper quietly.

"Going on one date doesn't mean we'll get married." I grab the kitchen towel off the counter and hand it to Mom to clean up her mess.

"How come?" Ezra asks, his bottom lip sticking out.

"Because . . . maybe we won't like each other that much. It takes time to fall in love, and Beau would have to love us both, or he's not the right guy for us."

He nods his head. "So, we have to get him to fall in love with you first. Everyone already loves me."

I laugh. "We'll see."

Mom finishes cleaning the mess she made and sits back in her chair. "Sometimes grown ups date and never fall in love. Sometimes they do. It just depends."

Ezra shakes his head. "He's gonna love Mommy. I just know it."

"All right, let's get dressed. What should we do today?"

Ezra jumps down from his chair and grins. "Let's go to the park!"

"It's raining," Mom says, pointing to the window. Sure enough, rain drops cling to the glass.

"Oh, man!" Ezra says, his little shoulders slumping.

"What if we go to the mall instead? Mommy can get a new outfit for her date, and you can play at the play area?" Mom asks.

"Yay!" Ezra takes off to his room to get dressed.

"I don't need a new outfit, Mom. I have clothes." Isn't one trip to the mall during the week of Christmas enough?

She smiles and pats my hand. "Of course you do, but a new outfit never hurts." She stands and takes her mug to the sink. "Besides, it will get Ezra out of the house and burn off a bit of that energy."

I give up. "Okay, I'll go get dressed."

"That's my girl."

Thirty minutes later, we're in the car and headed toward the mall. I say a little prayer that Elaine won't be there to ruin it this time. I can handle her talking to me like that, but I won't stand for her hurting Ezra. He's innocent and doesn't deserve to hear the mean things she has to say.

Mom puts on Christmas music and we sing along all the way to the mall. Ezra's little loud singing voice makes me smile. Being a single mom's not easy, but I wouldn't trade him for the world.

The rain has let up when we make it to the mall and park, so we are able to run inside without getting soaked. "I'll take him to the playground while you shop. Meet us there when you're done." Mom takes Ezra's hand in hers. "Ready to go play?"

Ezra jumps up and down. "Yep!"

"All right. Be good for Grandma. I'll look around, but I'm not promising anything," I say.

Mom smiles. "Take your time."

I watch as they head off in the direction of the play area. The small slide and climbing toys will keep him busy for a while. Where to start? I decide to head into Dillards. The clothes are always so soft and reasonably priced. Plus, they fit my curves just right, and that's not always easy to find.

"Welcome in," a young girl says, greeting me at the store's entrance. "Everything is forty percent off today. Let me know if you need help with anything. My name's Ira."

"Thanks," I say, moving to the right of the store. I wander around for a while before spotting a dark green dress hanging off to the side. It has long sleeves and is pulled in at the waist, then falls loosely to the floor. Its sweetheart neckline adds a soft, feminine touch, and the hidden pockets are a practical bonus. I grab my size and head for the dressing rooms.

Slipping the dress over my head, I sigh when it falls into place, hugging my hips just right without being tight or too revealing. I turn and look in the mirror, sucking in a breath when I see my reflection. The green of the dress brings out the green in my eyes, and it fits like it was made for me. I slide my hands into the pockets and grin. Plus, pockets! How can I say no?

Once I'm dressed again, I step out of the dressing room and head for the registers.

"Find everything okay?" Ira says as she rings me up.

"Yes, thank you." I take out my wallet and swipe my card.

"This dress is beautiful." She folds it neatly and slides it into a bag. "Merry Christmas."

I take the bag and the receipt, and smile. "Merry Christmas." Now to find Mom and Ezra. I head toward the indoor playground and stop when I pass a shoe store. In the window sits a cute pair of black ballet flats. The little bow on the top gives them a bit more personality. I head into the store to see if they have my size.

Twenty minutes later, I'm carrying two bags, and feeling more excited than nervous about the date tonight.

"I see you found something," Mom says when I join her on the bench inside the play area.

I nod. "I did. The dress is beautiful, and I got a pair of shoes, too."

Mom peeks in the bags. "Oh, that is pretty!"

"Ezra," I call getting his attention. He comes running over.

"Is it time to leave already?" he asks, whining.

"It is, but I thought we could stop in the food court for some lunch. What do you think?"

He runs over to the shoe cubby and grabs his shoes. "Come on, guys." He slips his feet into his sneakers and pulls the velcro straps tight. "I'm hungry."

Laughing, Mom and I follow a skipping Ezra toward the food court and his favorite pizza place.

"How mad do you think Aiden's going to be when he finds out?" I ask as we make our way through the crowd.

"He'll get over it," Mom says. "He's just being protective."

"I can handle him being upset with me, but Beau's his best friend." I sigh. "I don't want to come between them."

Mom wraps her arm around my shoulder and pulls me in. "You won't. Aiden won't let that happen."

I hope she's right.

Chapter Eight

Beau

I've avoided Aiden since Ashlan left this afternoon. How do you explain to your best friend that you've gone against his wishes and asked his little sister out on a date? Maybe I can just skip that part and let him find out on his own.

No. That's not right. I haven't lied to Aiden before, and I'm not going to start now. I'll just have to man up and tell him. Hopefully, I don't have a sore jaw for dinner tonight.

"Hey, man," I say, walking into the living room where Aiden's sitting on the couch scrolling through his phone. "Can I talk to you a sec?"

"That sounds ominous," Aiden says, setting his phone down on the arm of the sofa. "What's up?"

I rub my hands on my pants and resist the urge to start pacing. "Well, I have something to tell you and you're not going to like it."

Aiden shakes his head. "You didn't? Please, tell me you didn't."

"I did."

Aiden jumps up from his spot on the couch and paces around the room like a caged tiger at the zoo. "I specifically asked you not to go there."

I raise my hands in surrender. "I know."

"And, what? You just didn't care how I'd feel?" He runs his hands through his hair. "So much for being like brothers."

That stings. Aiden's the closest thing I have to family, and he knows it. "Aiden . . ."

He holds his hand up like a stop sign. "I can't believe this."

"I've liked her forever, you know that. The more time I spend with her . . . Aiden, I think I'm half in love with her already."

Aiden shakes his head and plops back down on the sofa. "I don't get it," he says, some of the fight draining out of him.

I shrug. "Me either. I thought when we left for college, the crush would go away."

He eyes me. "It didn't."

I shake my head. "It didn't. When I was home for my parents' funeral, it was like the smoldering crush blazed into a raging inferno. She was so caring, stopping by and offering to help with things. Bringing me food and sitting with me, and Ezra was adorable. Into everything and always babbling about something or another. He stole a piece of my heart then, too."

Aiden's mouth opens and closes. His jaw flexes like he's grinding his teeth. "You should have told me."

I shake my head. "Why? So you could freak out on me like this sooner? No thanks."

He laughs. "Yeah, I can't say I would have handled it any better."

"I'm sorry. Well, not about asking her out, but about upsetting you." I hold my breath waiting for him to respond. "Please, say something."

He shakes his head. "You'd really risk our friendship to date her?"

My heart sinks, but deep down, I know the answer. She's worth it. "I would."

Aiden smirks. "Okay then."

Wait, what? "'Okay' as in . . . ?"

"Okay as in I guess it's okay if you date her, but if you hurt her . . ." He shakes his head. "The thing is, TJ really did a number on her when he left like he did. His mom wasn't any better. Accusing her of sleeping around and refusing to acknowledge Ezra. Ashlan's got a world of responsibility on her shoulders." Aiden pins me with a look that makes me squirm in my seat. "Don't go there, unless you plan to go all in. Ezra doesn't need that, and she deserves someone who plans to give her the world. If you're not in it for the long haul . . . just back out now."

I can't find the words to respond, so I just nod.

"I'm going to bed." Aiden turns and walks inside, shutting the door behind him.

Well, that could have been worse.

*   *   *   *   *

"You still have a date with my sister?" Aiden asks when I enter the kitchen to get myself some coffee.

"Yeah, I do." I watch as emotions flicker across his face.

"When?"

"Tonight," I say, reaching for the pot and pouring myself the biggest mug I can find.

"You're sure you're ready for that?" he asks.

I nod and shrug. "It's one date."

He shakes his head. "Keep telling yourself that," he mumbles.

"What?" I ask.

"You two have liked each other for years. You really think this is going to be one date?"

My heart swells in my chest. No. I don't, but I'm afraid to get too far ahead of myself. "If she's not interested in me after tonight, it will be."

He eyes me, a pensive look on his face. "Good answer. Better get dressed, then."

I laugh. "What for?"

"We need to go to the mall." Aiden stands and heads to his room. "You need presents."

"I do?" I call after him. "For what?"

"You're not dating my sister and not giving her a Christmas present."

I hadn't even thought of that. What would I even get her? Obviously, I need to get something for Ezra as well. I can feel my anxiety rising. Taking a few deep breaths, I try to recenter. "Aiden, don't you think it's too soon for gift giving? We haven't even been on a date yet."

Aiden comes back down the hallway dressed in a nice pair of jeans and a light green sweater. "Wouldn't you want to give your girlfriend a present for Christmas?" he asks, raising an eyebrow and glaring at me.

"I don't have a girlfriend," I remind him. "We haven't been on a date yet." I can't start thinking of her like that yet. Not when I don't know if she's on the same page. Just because she agreed to dinner doesn't mean she wants more. I need to remember that.

"I know Ashlan," he says, moving to the couch to put on his shoes. "She isn't going to date someone she can't see herself with long term. Especially with Ezra in the picture. It's why she hasn't dated since he was born."

I frown. "At all?"

He smirks. "At all. Besides, I know you. You've wanted to be married and have a family since we were kids. You're not the date 'em and leave 'em kind."

"Thanks, I think."

He laughs. "You're welcome."

"Then, why were you so set on me not pursuing your sister?" I ask.

He pushes to standing and rolls his eyes. "Because it's weird. Why aren't you dressed?"

"Because I'm not going to the mall two days before Christmas, Aiden. Are you insane?" I shudder thinking about how packed it will be.

"No, but I'm sure you don't want to show up on Christmas with no presents. You want to win Ezra over, don't you?"

I hadn't really considered that. Dating a woman with a child is more complicated than I'd thought. "I guess so."

Aiden claps his hands together. "Great. Go get dressed."

An hour later, Aiden and I are walking through the mall, which is alive with holiday chaos—kids running wild, shoppers clutching overloaded bags, and Christmas music blasting just a little too loud. I give Aiden the side-eye only to see he's grinning like he's auditioning to be Santa's favorite elf or something.

"This is fun for you, isn't it?" I ask, weaving around a group of teenagers taking selfies in front of a giant tree.

"Absolutely," Aiden says, rubbing his hands together. "Making sure you don't blow it with my sister? Epic. I have to make sure you don't get her something practical, like a toaster or something."

What's wrong with practical? "I wouldn't get her a toaster. I'm not a complete moron," I say. Though, I had been thinking about a new pair of sneakers. I'm sure Aiden knows her size, or their mom does. I'd noticed the coffee stains on the ones she left by the door when we'd been over for dinner. Now, though, Aiden has me second guessing myself.

"Okay, Romeo," Aiden says. "What did you have in mind?"

"Honestly? New sneakers," I reply.

Aiden snorts and slaps my back. "It's a good thing I'm here. You need more help than I thought."

I don't know whether to be relieved Aiden seems on board now, or worried he's lulling me into a false sense of security before punching me in the face.

"Come on," Aiden says, pointing to a store filled with candles and lotions. "Maybe there's something in here."

I pick up a holiday-themed gift set, giving it a sniff, the gingerbread scent making me sneeze. Grabbing another, I decide the warm cranberry spice smells much better and hold it out to Aiden. "Does this say 'I like you' or 'I panic-bought this because I didn't know what else to get you?'"

Aiden winces. "It says she's your grandma. Next."

After walking through three stores, I've nearly given up. Everything I pick up isn't right, according to Aiden. "You have to get her something meaningful, but not over the top." He makes a face when I hold up a Christmas sweater. "And definitely not something you'd give your mom if she were still here."

"Can we get something to eat?" I ask, putting the sweater back on the rack. "I think I'm going to need to refuel before we go to any more stores."

Aiden laughs. "Sure, but you're buying."

Fine by me. We make our way to the food court, scooting around window-shoppers and dodging a kid wielding a giant candy cane. Finally, we make it. "What do you feel like?" I ask.

Aiden points to the pizza place. "Pizza, man. It's the only safe mall food."

I chuckle and follow him to the line.

"Hey," I hear a small voice shout. "Uncle Aiden!"

I turn in time to see Ezra take off running in our direction. Ashlan and her mom are hot on his heels.

"Well, fancy seeing you here," Aiden says, scooping Ezra up and hugging him tight. "What are you guys doing at the mall?"

"Mom's buying a new dress for her date."

I grin and glance up at Ashlan. Maybe she's as excited as I am after all.

"Ezra," Ashlan says when they reach us. "You can't just run off."

"I didn't," he says, wiggling in Aiden's arms. "I went to Uncle Aiden."

"Next time, walk, please," Mrs. Dewitt says. "What are you boys doing at the mall?"

I look at Aiden, begging him with my eyes to not say anything. Apparently he sees "Embarrass me, please" instead.

"We're buying Beau here new underwear." Ezra giggles. "Just kidding. I'm helping him pick out some presents for Ashlan and Ezra."

"Oh, that's lovely," Mrs. Dewitt says, grinning from ear to ear. "How thoughtful."

Ashlan's beet red, clearly embarrassed as well. "You don't need to do that," she says, shifting her weight to pick up Ezra.

"Yes he does," Aiden says. "If he wants to date my little sister, he's got to treat you both right."

I shake my head. "I wanted to," I say. "Though I could have avoided this fun interaction if I'd just left Aiden at home."

"Yeah," Aiden scoffs, "but then you'd have gotten her some stinky lotion or something lame."

Ashlan chuckles. "I happen to like lotion," she says pointedly.

Aiden rolls his eyes. "Then buy it for yourself. That's not a boyfriend gift, that's a gift from your mom."

"*Boyfriend* gift? I think you're getting ahead of yourself," Ashlan says, her eyes search mine—for what, I don't know. I'd love to be her boyfriend, but it seems really fast to make that assumption. Ezra's watching us, absorbing this entire conversation. The last thing I'd want to do is hurt him.

"You two . . ." Aiden says, sighing heavily. "Fine, but when it's official, I'm going to say I told you so."

Mrs. Dewitt laughs. "Leave them alone. Weren't you the one a few days ago flipping out that they may like each other?"

"Well, yeah," Aiden says. "But that was a few days ago. Before he asked her out." He pins me with a look I can't quite decipher. "Now that we've talked some, I'm on board. Or trying to be. Besides, what could be better than having my best friend for a brother-in-law? Beats some deadbeat trying to win her and Ezra's hearts."

Mrs. Dewitt shakes her head. "Very mature of you."

"Next," the lady behind the counter calls, forcing everyone to drop this conversation and order food.

Once everyone has ordered, we search the packed dining area for a table big enough for all five of us. It takes a minute, but Aiden finds a group about to leave and snags theirs. "Here," he says, pulling out the chair beside him. "Ezra, you can sit by me."

Ezra hops up into the chair and swings his legs.

I set the trays I'm carrying down on the table, and Ashlan passes out the food. "Thanks," she says when everyone's eating. "You didn't need to pay for lunch."

"No problem," I say. "I'd already told Aiden I was buying."

Aiden and Ezra are discussing the intelligence of octopuses, and I can't help but laugh at Ezra's enthusiasm. "Sounds like you really know your sea animals," I say when there's a break in the conversation.

"I do. I want to go to the ocean and swim with them, but Mom says it's too far away." He frowns.

"Hmm. Maybe one day you'll get there," I say, looking at Ashlan.

"Maybe," she agrees. "If the ocean magically moves closer to Arkansas."

I don't mention that I could book a trip this week. That's too soon. But, I find my mind wandering to thoughts of a family vacation on the beach. Taking Ezra swimming and walking along the beach picking up shells. I glance at Ashlan, and smile. Maybe one day . . .

After lunch, we part ways, and I head for the toy store. Since I helped wrap all the presents Aiden and Ashlan already bought, I know they didn't get anything octopus-related, and after the conversation today, I'm sure Ezra would love something like that.

I search the aisles until I come across a stuffed octopus and toss it in the cart.

"Oh, good one," Aiden says. "Hard to wrap, but he'll love it."

"That's what gift bags are for," I say, stopping when I spot an ocean puzzle. "Do you think he could do this?" The box says six plus, but it seems like a lot of pieces, so I'm not sure.

"I'm sure he could, and if he can't, Mom and Ash would help him."

I toss it into the cart and look for puzzle glue. "We need a frame for it. When he's done, they can glue it together and frame it for his room."

"Oh, that's a great idea, actually." Aiden grabs a bottle of puzzle glue and tosses it into the cart. "We can hit Walmart on the way home for a frame."

I nod. "Good idea."

"Now, what are you getting for Ash?"

That's just it. I'm still not sure what to get her. Hopefully something comes to me soon. Otherwise, I'm going back for that lotion.

Chapter Nine

Ashlan

"Wow, Mommy," Ezra says when I enter the living room at a quarter till six. "You look like a princess."

"Thank you," I tell him, swooping down and giving his face kisses.

Giggling, he squirms away. "Stop, Mommy. You're getting lipstick on my face."

"Okay, I'll stop," I say. "Are you going to be good for Grandma tonight?"

His little eyes light up and he bobs his head up and down. "Yep! We're going to make cookies for Santa, and watch *The Grinch*!"

I ruffle his light brown hair. "My favorite." I glance at the cuckoo clock. It's nearly six and nerves have been turning my stomach to knots for the last hour and a half.

The doorbell rings, and I suck in a deep breath. "Is that Beau?" Ezra asks, running to the living room window and pulling back the curtains.

Mom breezes by us to the door. "Let's find out," she says, opening it wide. "Why, hello," she says, turning and winking at Ezra. "I think it's for you, Ashlan."

Mom steps back and motions for Beau to come inside. "Whoa," Ezra says loudly. "You look like a prince."

He's not wrong. Gone are the worn jeans and flannel shirts, and in their place is a beautifully tailored black suit.

"Thanks," Beau says, his eyes on mine. "I wanted to look nice." He breaks eye contact and moves over to where Ezra is standing by the recliner. "Here," he says, passing him a small toy. "It's a puzzle box. There's supposed to be over seventy different shapes you can make."

"Cool!" Ezra says, taking the small toy. "Thanks!"

"You're welcome," Beau says, holding his hand out for a high five. Ezra happily obliges and runs off to the living room to play with his new toy.

Beau steps back out onto the porch and comes back inside holding a dozen roses. "And these are for you." He passes me the bouquet and puts his hands behind his back. "I didn't know your favorites or anything, so I just got the first date standard."

I laugh at his admission. "Thanks, they're beautiful."

"I'll just put these in some water for you," Mom says, taking the bouquet and nudging us toward the door. "You two should probably get going."

"I just need to say bye to Ezra," I say, trying to get around Mom, who is now effectively blocking my way.

"Bye, Mom," Ezra calls. "Be good."

Mom chuckles. "You heard the kid. Go on. Have a nice time."

I shake my head. "Thanks, Mom."

Beau moves back, waiting for me to step outside before following me out the door and down the steps to his truck. "Here," he says, moving quickly to the door. "Let me get that for you."

He opens the door and offers his hand to help me climb up into the cab. "Thank you." He smiles and shuts the door carefully. While he makes his way to the driver's side, I snap my seat belt into place and take a deep breath. How long has it been since someone opened my car door for me? Forever. TJ would never have done something so sweet.

"So," Beau says, climbing up and starting the ignition. "I hope you like steak." My stomach chooses that moment to growl, and he chuckles. "I'll take that as a yes."

I laugh along with him. "I do like steak, thanks."

He makes small talk, asking me about Ezra and the coffee shop as we drive along. I expected the drive to feel awkward, but it doesn't. Conversation flows easily between us. When he pulls into the parking lot of Cattleman's Steakhouse, my mouth starts to water. The restaurant is only about twenty minutes outside of town, but it's a bit on the pricey side, so I don't get to eat here often.

"You didn't need to bring me somewhere so nice," I say after he opens my door and helps me out of the truck. "I'm a simple girl. I could have eaten at Beats and Eats and been just fine."

He shrugs. "You deserve nice things, too, Ash. Besides, I wanted steak, and we both know the diner isn't the place to get a good steak. Fried chicken, yes . . . steak, not so much." He raises an eyebrow like he's daring me to disagree.

I raise my hands in surrender. "You're not wrong about that," I say, agreeing with him.

"Good, so let's go eat some steak, shall we?" He places his hand at the small of my back and guides me to the heavy wooden doors. The hostess pushes the door open and holds it for us as we step inside.

The restaurant is everything you'd expect an upscale steakhouse to be. Black tablecloths cover solid wood tables. Each table displays a small glass globe candle, creating a romantic ambiance.

"Table for two?" the hostess asks, drawing my attention away from the wagon wheels and other western memorabilia on the walls.

"Yes, please," Beau says. "Reservation is under 'Travers.'"

She nods and grabs two menus. "Right this way, please." We follow her through the dining room and to a table for two along the back wall. "Will this be okay?"

Beau nods and pulls out my chair, waiting for me to sit before gently pushing it in and taking his seat on the opposite side. "Thank you."

"Your server will be right over," she says, laying the menus on the table in front of us.

I glance at the menu and my eyes nearly bug out of my head. There's a steak listed for a hundred dollars!

"Don't worry about the price," Beau says, a soft smile on his face. "I can afford it."

"If you're sure," I reply, carefully scanning the menu for the cheapest meal option.

"And don't skimp out either. I want you to enjoy yourself." He pins me with a knowing look. "Please, get what you want."

"Okay," I say, relenting. The steak does smell delicious and my mouth is already watering.

"Hello," a woman says, approaching the table. "My name's Susie, and I'll be taking care of you tonight. Would you care to start out with a glass of wine?"

I shake my head. "No thank you. Water with lemon, please."

She nods and turns to Beau. "And for you, sir?"

"I'll have water as well."

"I'll have this out for you in just a moment."

After she leaves to get our drinks, we take our time discussing the menu options. By the time she's back, I've decided on the filet while he chose the ribeye. Susan takes our order and assures us the food will be out shortly.

"Did I tell you how beautiful you look?" Beau asks.

A gentle smile tugs at my lips. "I think so, but you can tell me again . . . just to be sure."

He chuckles. "You're stunning, but then again, you always take my breath away."

My insides melt like an ice cube on the sidewalk in the heat of summer. "Why, Beau Travers, are you sweet on me?" I ask in my best southern accent.

He grins and plays along. "Ms. Ashlan, I don't reckon there's a finer sight in all the world than you right here before me. I'd be mighty honored if you'd let me court you."

We burst out laughing, and just like that, the first date jitters disappear.

"How's the cabin coming along?" I ask. I was there yesterday, but I was so focused on Beau that I didn't really look around.

"It's going," he says, taking a sip of his water. "Aiden and I finished staining the living area, so that's done. I've been working on the walls in my room. I'd love to start on the outside, but it's too cold. I'll have to wait for spring."

"What else are you planning to do?" I listen as Beau tells me about his plans for the cabin and can't help but imagine what it would be like to live there. Away from the noise of the city and Old Mrs. Crane shaking her cane at anyone who makes noise after seven p.m.

"Here we are," Susie says, setting my plate in front of me, then doing the same with Beau's. "Enjoy."

I cut into my steak and pop a bite into my mouth. I can't help the small sound that escapes my lips. "It's so good," I say, after I swallow my bite.

Beau shifts in his chair and smiles. "I'm glad you like it."

We take turns talking about everything and nothing while we eat. Reminiscing on some of the antics he and Aiden got up to as kids. My cheeks hurt from smiling so much, and I feel like I'm floating on air. Is this what dating Beau will be like? If so, it's even better than I imagined.

Chapter Ten

Beau

By the time we share dessert—cherry cheesecake—I'm fully in love with this woman. Ashlan's strong, funny, beautiful, kind . . . everything I have ever wanted in a partner.

Watching her eat her steak and potato was a refreshing change from the few women I'd taken out in Austin who insisted on picking at a salad all night. I never could understand that.

When Susie drops off our bill, I slip cash inside the little book. "Ready to go?" I ask Ashlan.

She sighs. "Yeah, I suppose it's time."

I can't help but grin at her reluctance to end our date. I stand and offer my hand to her. She takes it and links her fingers through mine as we walk through the restaurant and out to the truck. "Thank you for joining me tonight," I say, when I help her up into the cab. "I had a great time."

"Me too," she says, a light pink staining her cheeks.

Once we are both settled in the truck and the heat is blowing, I pull out of the parking lot and head towards her house. "I'd like to see you again," I say, putting the ball in her court.

"I mean, you'll see me again anyway, won't you?" she teases.

I chuckle. "You're right, but I mean I'd love to take you out again. Maybe we can take Ezra next time. I'd love to take him to the Blue Zoo Aquarium over in Rogers."

I feel her looking at me, but I don't look away from the road. If she's going to reject me, I don't want to watch it happen. I've liked her from afar for far too long. If she's not interested, it will hurt, but I'd rather be in her life as a friend than not at all.

"That would be amazing," she says finally. "I just . . . Are you sure about this? I mean, I'm a lot."

I glance in her direction and notice her worrying her hands together. Flipping on my blinker, I pull onto the shoulder of the road and turn to her. "You are not a lot. You are perfect."

She snorts. "You haven't been around much these last few years to know how imperfect I really am. I'm a single mom, with a deadbeat baby daddy. I still live at home with my mom, and I have no idea how to be everything that little boy needs. I hardly ever dress up," she says, waving her hands over her dress, "and I'm moody when I don't eat."

She pauses to suck in a breath.

"Are you done?" I ask, trying to keep the smile off my face.

"No, I haven't even gotten started," she says, shaking her head.

I can't contain the laugh anymore. "Woman," I say, trying to get myself together. "I know all that. Over the years, I've gotten as much information from Aiden as I could without arousing his suspicions. I've liked you since we were in high school. When Aiden and I left for college, I thought that teen crush would go away. Spoiler alert, it didn't. The next time I saw you, though, you were with that schmuck and it took everything I had to stay out of it."

Her mouth drops open, and her eyes widen in surprise. "Oh," she says quietly.

"Yeah. Oh. Those conversations we had when I was home for Mom and Dad's funeral; that time we spent together just talking after Aiden had gone back to Austin? The highlight of my life. I wanted so badly to ask you out then, but the timing felt all wrong. Our business had just gotten off the ground and was taking up all my time. Plus, I knew Aiden would pop a gasket."

She nods her head. "I thought you might have liked me back then, but when you didn't come back home, and Aiden talked about the women you were dating, I figured you didn't want a small town girl with a child."

I rub my hands down my face. Of course Aiden would talk about the dates. "Did Aiden happen to tell you most of those dates were double dates that he set up because he liked her friend and wanted to get me out of the house?"

She crunched her nose up with a grin. "Nope. He left that part out."

"Somehow I figured." I've been half in love with Ashlan since high school, but staying away had felt like the only option. She was off-limits. I value my friendship with Aiden. He is family, and the unspoken code between brothers might as well have been carved in stone.

When college came, I convinced myself that putting distance between us was for the best. Especially once she had Ezra. She needed someone who was ready to settle down and devote his time to a family, and that wasn't me. Not then.

If I'm being brutally honest—I was scared too. If I confessed my feelings and things fell apart, I'd lose not only her but the family I had in Aiden. So, I kept my distance.

After college, staying away had become a habit. I tried dating other women, but no one ever measured up. Now, after being around her again, I can't help but wonder if maybe I've been wrong to stay away. Maybe I should have taken the risk years ago. I've been a coward. I just hope it's not too late.

We sit in the quiet of the cab for a moment. Both lost in our own thoughts.

"So, what now?" she asks in a small voice.

I shift in the seat so I'm facing her. "That's entirely up to you," I reply. "I would love to take this further and explore a relationship with you and Ezra, but if you're not on board with that . . . I'm happy to remain friends instead."

She looks out the window, and my heart races. I wasn't even this nervous when we were approached about selling our software company.

Finally, she turns and meets my eyes. "I'm worried. What if it doesn't work out? What if you decide we *are* too much?"

I swallow hard, taking my time to respond so she knows I'm serious. "What if it does work out? What if this is our last first date?"

She smiles, and her eyes glisten. "I'm being serious," she says.

"Me too." I watch as her face displays every thought going through her pretty head. When I see she's not going to respond, I say, "I think my option is far more likely than yours. I've thought about this. Ezra's a cute kid. He's yours. I care about you, therefore, I care about him." I shrug. "Families aren't always made up of biological parents and kids. They're people who love each other, regardless."

A single tear slips down her cheek and I reach over and gently wipe it off. "It's up to you, and you don't have to decide tonight." I wait until she nods before flipping the blinker on and moving back onto the road. "I was thinking. Aiden and I can sneak the presents over tomorrow after Ezra goes to bed. Does that work for you?"

She nods. "That would be perfect. I forgot about the other presents!"

I snicker. "Don't worry about it. Aiden and I finished up."

Her eyebrows rise and she breaks into laughter. "Oh, this should be good."

Grinning, I look over and feign hurt. "Are you saying my wrapping skills are subpar? I happen to have a very good teacher, ma'am."

"I bet they're perfect," she says, trying and failing to keep a straight face.

"Well, we'll just have to see what Ezra thinks, won't we?"

"I suppose so, Mr. Elf. Will you be joining us for Christmas? I know Mom told Aiden to invite you."

"I haven't really celebrated much since my parents died."

She reaches out and places a hand on my shoulder. The warmth of her palm seeps through the suit jacket I'm wearing and right into my heart. "We would love to have you. I know Mr. and Mrs. Travers would have wanted you to celebrate."

"Yeah," I say, swallowing back emotion. "Mom would have my hide for avoiding the holiday she loved most."

Ashlan squeezes my shoulder and lets her hand drop back into her lap. "It's up to you, but I know I, for one, would like you there. Besides, Ezra made you a gift."

My heart leaps in my chest. That has to be a good sign, right? "He did?"

She nods. "He is very much into the gift-giving spirit this year. I've never had to clean up so much glitter in my life."

I chuckle. "Sounds like I have to come now."

"Only if you want to," she says, her tone serious.

Ten minutes later, I pull into her driveway, and I'm surprised to see Aiden's truck in the drive. I park behind him and turn off the truck. Turning, I reach for her hands and hold them in mine. "I'd love to. It's time."

Her eyes hold mine, and I am overcome with the desire to lean forward and place my lips on hers. I start to move, and then pull back. She hasn't decided if she's ready to continue seeing me as more than friends, and I need to respect that.

I squeeze her hands in mine. "I had a great time with you tonight."

"Me too." She leans closer to me and places a soft kiss on my cheek, right as the porch lights flip on and Aiden steps out the front door.

"What are you two kids getting up to out there?" he calls, wagging a finger in the air.

Ashlan and I share a look and burst out laughing. "I guess that means it's time to walk you to your door."

I slip out of the truck and head to her side, helping her down and reluctantly letting her go when her feet are on solid ground.

"Think about it," I say softly. "It's your call."

She nods and heads to where Aiden is tapping his foot. "You're late," he says playfully, pulling her in for a hug. "I hope this knucklehead took care of you?"

She glances over her shoulder and smiles. "Mind your business," she mutters before pushing past him and heading inside.

I sputter with laughter as Aiden mumbles something about protecting her honor. "You know she's safe with me."

He nods. "I do, but that doesn't mean I'm not going to be a pain in the butt." He grins. "So, how was it? Did you land a second date?"

I pinch my fingers together and motion like I'm zipping my lips.

Aiden throws his hands up in the air. "Is no one going to tell me anything?"

"No," Mrs. Dewitt says, coming to the door. "Now be quiet before old Mrs. Crane comes out waving her cane."

Aiden laughs. "Fair enough." He leans in and places a kiss on his mom's cheek. "We'll be by tomorrow for dinner and to bring the presents."

She nods. "Good. Now, unless you're here for anything other than bothering me on purpose, go home." She waves to me and closes the door in Aiden's face.

"Man, some people . . ."

"This has been one of the best nights of my life," I say, walking back to my truck and leaving Aiden standing on the porch. Hopefully, there are many more to come.

Chapter Eleven

Ashlan

"Come on, Mom," Ezra says, jumping on my bed. "We need to get there early and get a good spot."

I groan. The Christmas Eve parade is always the highlight of the day for Ezra. Seeing the town come together and decorate trucks, trailers, and golf carts with Christmas cheer makes him squeal with delight. I just wish it started a bit later than nine in the morning. "I'm coming. Are you and Grandma ready?"

"Yep!" he says, bouncing down to his bottom on the bed and hopping down. "Grandma said to tell you to hurry up."

I sit up and wipe the sleep from my eyes. After last night's date, I was floating on air and way too adrenaline-filled to fall asleep at a decent hour. Instead, I'd stayed up replaying everything Beau had said.

"Come on!" Ezra says, pulling the blankets down. "Santa's coming to town."

"Okay," I say, sliding out of bed and heading into the bathroom. "I'll be ready in ten minutes."

He groans, but I hear his little feet pad down the hallway. Thank goodness Mom's an early riser and doesn't mind getting up with Ezra on my days off. Otherwise, I'd be a permanently exhausted mess.

"Here," Mom says, passing me a travel mug of steaming hot coffee. "I figured you might need this."

I take the cup and bring it to my nose, inhaling the rich scent of caffeine. "Thanks."

I follow her and Ezra to the car and slip into the passenger seat.

"So," Mom says, before she's even pulled out of the driveway. "How was last night?"

I look over my shoulder and smile at Ezra. "Later," I say.

Mom frowns, but nods her head.

"Mommy, how does Santa come to our house if we don't have a chimney?" Ezra asks from the back seat.

"What?" I ask, buying time. I'm so not awake enough for this.

"We don't have a chimney, but in the stories and movies, Santa comes down the chimney to leave presents."

I nod, trying to come up with an answer that might satisfy him.

"And how come he doesn't burn his butt?" he follows up.

Mom bubbles with laughter beside me, and shakes her head indicating I'm on my own with this one.

"Well, I think Santa has some special pants that keep his butt from burning." Yeah, that sounds good.

"Like firemans wear?"

"Probably," I say, hoping that talking about fireproof pants will derail his first question.

"That makes sense." He glances out the window, his face scrunched up in thought. "But how can he get in if we don't have a chimney?"

So, his train of thought is still right on track.

"Santa has a special key," Mom pipes in. "It helps him open doors."

I mouth "Thank you" at her and she winks back.

"Okay," Ezra says, pulling out his favorite fidget toy.

"We're here," Mom says, maneuvering into an empty space in the old bank parking lot. "Looks like Aurora's saved a spot for us in front of the Coffee Loft."

"It pays to have an awesome boss," I say, opening the door for Ezra and taking his hand so he doesn't run off. "Ezra, help me get the chairs out of the trunk and we can get some hot cocoa from Ms. Aurora."

A few minutes later, we're seated in front of the coffee shop, hot cocoas and s'mores muffins in hand, awaiting the parade.

"At least tell me if you plan to see him again," Mom says when Ezra starts dancing to the drum beat from the local high school marching band warming up down the way.

"I don't know. It's complicated." My eyes dance in amusement when other little kids join Ezra and dance along the sidewalk.

"Is it really?" Mom asks and starts listing things on her fingers. "You like each other. You've known each other for years. You're already friends. He's a total catch, and so are you. Seems to me it's the least complicated situation you could hope for."

"That's just it. He's Aiden's best friend. What if we fight? I don't want Aiden to feel like he has to choose sides. Or worse, what if he tries to get in the middle of it? What happens if Beau decides taking on someone else's child is too much for him?" I shake my head. "It's a lot."

"You're letting fear win," Mom says, tapping her finger on my nose. "Remember how scared you were when TJ walked away and you were facing parenthood on your own?"

I shudder. "How could I forget?"

"You were certain you wouldn't be a good mom, but look at him." She points to Ezra laughing hysterically as he and Matti clap their hands to the beat. "Does that look like a kid who's being raised by a bad mom?"

"I've had help," I say, nudging her.

"We all have help in life. That's how it works. But ultimately, he's your son, and you're the one raising him. Don't let fear hold you back from something great."

"I'll think about it." Thankfully I'm saved from continuing the conversation as the Piney Brook High marching band starts making its way down the street. We watch as each vehicle passes, decorated with snowmen, gingerbread houses, and—Ezra's favorite—a Santa shark, then finally the golf cart carrying Mr. and Mrs. Claus, a.k.a. Mr. and Mrs. Crane, passes by. I laugh as Ezra waves so hard his whole body wiggles.

"Ready to go to the park?" I ask, packing up the chairs.

"Can Matti come too?" Ezra asks.

"That's up to his mommy and daddy," I reply. Since Matti has been living with Knox and Lacey, he's taken to calling his biological parents Mom and Dad, and them Mommy and Daddy. It's sweet and I know it means a lot to them. Lacey gives me a thumbs up and says they'll meet us there.

After loading the chairs back into the trunk, we walk over to the park and I let Ezra free on the playground while Mom stays behind chatting with some of her friends.

"Thanks for inviting us," Lacey says, taking Matti's coat and watching him run to join Ezra on the swings. "Knox has to go into the hospital for a while today, and he's a bundle of energy this morning."

I laugh. "I know what you mean." We watch as the boys swing, kicking their little legs as hard as they can.

"Mommy, watch me!" Matti calls.

"I'm watching," Lacey calls back, beaming. Matti jumps from the swing, landing on his feet and claps his hands. "Good job!"

"Was it hard for you?" I ask. "You know, stepping in to help raise a kid that wasn't yours?"

Lacey turns to face me and shakes her head. "Not really. I love kids and Matti's the sweetest. It took some time to settle into the role of caregiver in a new way. I'd started out as his nanny, you know, but no. I don't even think of him as not mine anymore. Of course, we honor his parents, and spend time each day talking about them, so he knows how loved he was, but he's mine in every way that counts."

I sit back on the bench and mull over what she's shared. Her situation is a bit different, of course, but I always wondered if it would be hard for someone else to see Ezra as their own. Especially since his biological father wants nothing to do with him.

"Is there a reason you're asking?" Lacey asks, a knowing grin on her face. "Does that mean the rumors are true? You and Beau . . ."

"We've been on *one* date."

"How was it?" Lacey asks.

"Yeah," Mom says, walking up and taking a seat beside me. "How was the date?"

I relay the events of the previous evening, and by the end, they are both grinning like loons. "He says it's up to me," I finish.

Lacey squeals a bit before schooling her features. "It sounds to me like he's already considered whether he feels comfortable taking on a child, and has decided he does."

"Yeah, but how can he be sure? The idea of parenting is way different than actually being in it all the time."

Mom pats my leg. "You have to trust him and communicate. Follow your gut."

"My gut's not always reliable. Otherwise, I wouldn't have ended up with TJ to begin with."

Mom rolls her eyes. "Oh, please. Can you honestly say you didn't know he was bad news?"

I think about that. Had I known it? There'd been signs he wasn't "the one" from the beginning, but I figured we were young and he'd mature. Ugh. I did know. "You're right." I sigh. "I knew, but I thought he would change. Especially when I found out that I was expecting."

Lacey shakes her head. "When people show you who they are, believe them."

I don't respond since I'm not sure what to say to that. I think back to the time I spent with Beau when his parents died. He was grieving, but he also got on the floor and played with Ezra, laughing and having a good time with him. He is a good man. I know that. The part I don't know is if I'm brave enough to take a chance.

Chapter Twelve

Beau

"I THINK THIS IS the last of it," Aiden says, his breath clouding in the crisp air. He puts the stack of presents in the truck. "Maybe I did overdo it just a bit."

"You think?" I ask, moving the presents out of the passenger seat and climbing into the warm cab. "Now I get to ride all the way to your mom's with a lap full of stuff."

Aiden grins. "'Uncle of the Year' award is coming my way. Ezra deserves a great Christmas."

"I suppose you're right. I mean, how many Christmases do you get where they still believe in the magic of Santa? Ten? Twelve?"

Aiden shakes his head. "These days, I bet it's a lot earlier than that when they stop believing." He climbs in and shuts the door, warming his hands in front of the vent.

"Well, that's kind of sad," I say, remembering my own childhood and how magical it was to wake up to presents from the jolly man himself.

Aiden shrugs, his expression turning thoughtful. "I guess that's why we have to do it up now." He pulls out of the driveway and starts down the mountain, the presents shifting in the back of the extended cab.

"I hope your future wife has the same mentality, or you're going to be in hot water buying so much."

Aiden bursts out laughing. "Dude, don't act like you're not impressed! This haul is legendary."

Considering I haven't celebrated Christmas in two years, who am I to judge how many presents Aiden should buy his nephew? My parents went the "less is more" route and focused on experience gifts over toys. It was still magical, just in a different way.

Aiden rounds a corner, and the precariously stacked presents in the back slide, launching a colorfully wrapped box towards the front of the truck. I lunge, dropping the presents from my lap onto the floor and catch the one from the back just before it connects with Aiden's head.

"Whoa," Aiden says. "Nice catch. Thanks."

"I'm just glad I caught it and we didn't get to try out these fancy new airbags tonight."

Aiden snorts. "I guess I didn't think about packing the truck to the ceiling being a bad idea."

I stick my arm behind me, holding the presents back. "Next time, we'll take two cars."

Thankfully, the rest of the trip is uneventful. The colorful Christmas lights on the houses in town make me smile. Maybe I'll decorate the cabin next year after all. It seems silly since no one but me will be out there to see it, but it's nice to look at.

Aiden pulls into the driveway at Mrs. Dewitt's and turns off the truck. "Here," he says, reaching out and adjusting the stack of boxes I'd been holding back. "That should work for now. We'll get them out after Ezra's in bed."

Picking up the boxes from the floor, I pass them to him to hold. "I'll get out and you can put those back in the seat."

"Hey, boys," Ashlan calls from the front porch. "Are you coming in, or do you plan to sit in the truck all night?"

Aiden shakes his head. "Always giving me a hard time, huh, Ash?"

She shrugs. "Someone has to do it."

Ashlan's dark brown hair's pulled back in a bun, and she's wearing the most adorable oversized sweater that says "Powered by Coffee and Christmas Cheer" over leggings covered in Christmas mugs. She looks relaxed and happy. She takes my breath away. "You look beautiful," I say quietly as I pass her to enter the house.

"If you say so," she calls back.

"If he says what?" Aiden asks, stepping past her and into the house.

"Nothing," she says, winking at me, which causes my heart to pound furiously in my chest. "Come on. Mom's in the kitchen."

We follow her into the kitchen where Ezra's on a little stool mixing something in a big bowl. "Uncle Aiden," he shouts, hopping down and launching himself into Aiden's arms.

"Hey, squirt," Aiden says, holding him tight. "Who's your favorite uncle?"

Ezra giggles and rolls his little eyes and looks so much like his mom for a moment. "You're my only uncle."

Aiden grins. "That makes me the favorite!" He tickles Ezra before setting him on his feet again.

"Hi, Beau," Ezra says, reaching his little fist out for a fist bump. We tap fists and do the hand explosion before he hops back on the stool and starts mixing again.

"What are you making?" I ask, moving closer to where he's working.

"Pancake mix," he says, his little tongue sticking out the side of his mouth. "It's almost done."

"Nice. I love pancakes." Aiden's family has had a pancake breakfast for Christmas Eve dinner as long as I've known them. "I can't wait to try yours!"

"Here," Mrs. Dewitt says, handing Aiden a tray of bacon and sausage. "Can you put that on the table, please?"

He leans in and pecks her cheek. "Anything for you, Ma."

She points to a tray of cut fruit. "Can you take that to the table, Beau? We'll be out in five."

Grabbing the platter, I turn and slam right into Aiden who has to be a superhero to be back in the kitchen so fast. Fruit goes flying, and Ezra gasps. "Oh no, the strawberries!"

I'm frozen in shock. "I'm so sorry," I finally manage. Aiden's picking sliced bananas from his shirt. Poor Ezra's in tears, and Ashlan is standing in the space between the dining room and the kitchen, holding the meat platter, with a look of pure disbelief on her face. Not the impression I'd hoped to make tonight.

Suddenly, Mrs. Dewitt doubles over in laughter, breaking the tension and causing everyone else to join in, including Ezra, who's now sniffle-laughing. "It's okay. We have more fruit, but the look on your faces . . ." She wipes tears away, still chuckling. "Priceless."

"I'll grab more fruit while you two clean this up," Ashlan says, setting the bacon on the table and pointing between me and her brother.

By the time Aiden and I have tracked down every errant blueberry and smashed banana, Ashlan's remade the fruit tray, and the pancakes are on the table.

"Let's settle down and eat," Mrs. Dewitt says, patting my cheek. "I'm sure you're starving after all that."

"So," Ezra says, digging into the pancakes Ashlan cut up on his plate. "Are you my mommy's boyfriend now?"

Aiden holds his hand up for a high five. "Way to ask the important questions, E."

"Uh," I stammer. "That's . . . that's really up to your mom." Ashlan's eyes are wide, and I feel bad for passing that one to her, but it's true. It's her call.

"Well?" Aiden asks, clearly enjoying everyone's discomfort.

"You're worse than Ezra," Ashlan mutters.

"Thanks!" Aiden says, taking another bite of his pancake.

"That wasn't a compliment." She takes a deep breath and looks at Ezra who is still waiting patiently for an answer. "We are still figuring that part out," she says, side-eyeing me.

I nod and give her what I hope is an encouraging smile.

"Okay," Ezra says, going back to his breakfast.

The rest of the meal passes in quiet chatter, with Ashlan and Aiden taking every opportunity to rib each other. I swear, these two are like teenagers when they're together. I guess some things never change. Being an only child, I never got to experience that sibling bickering they seem to have down to a science.

"Is it time for presents?" Ezra asks once the table's cleared and the kitchen's cleaned up.

"Sure," Ashlan says, "but go put on your pajamas and brush your teeth first."

"Aw, Mom!" he complains.

She raises an eyebrow in his direction and he heads down the hallway to do as she asked.

"He's a good kid," I say when he disappears into his room.

She nods. "Yeah, I got lucky."

A few minutes later, Aiden and Mrs. Dewitt are sitting on the love seat, and Ashlan and I are across the living room on the sofa. Ezra takes his time looking at the presents under the tree before finally choosing one and sitting down on the floor.

"What do you think it is?" Ashlan asks as he shakes the box.

"New pants," he guesses, tearing into the wrapping paper. "Hey!" he shouts. "A new coloring book with sharks and fish! Thanks, Mom!"

Ashlan laughs. "That was from Grandma."

"Thanks, Grandma!" He jumps up from his spot on the floor like only a five-year-old can manage, and rushes over to give his grandma a hug.

"You're welcome." She holds him tight for a few minutes before letting him go. "Want to go get the book?" she asks.

He nods his head and runs down the hallway.

"Walk," Ashlan calls after him, but it's too late. He's already running back, a stack of picture books in his hands.

"Here," he says, handing them to me. "You can read this time, but you have to show the pictures."

I take the books from his hands and nod. "I can do that." I flip the first book over and show the front cover before opening to the first page and reading. Twenty minutes later, I'm on the last page of *The Night Before Christmas*. When I turn the book to show him the picture, I see Ezra fast asleep on Ashlan. My heart skips a beat and I can't help but picture her with more children in the future. Suddenly, I want that more than anything in the world. "I haven't heard that story since I was a kid," I say, tugging myself from my daydream.

Ashlan smiles. "It's a tradition around here. Plus, it helps Ezra fall asleep." She scoots carefully out from under him and stands. "One of these days, I'm not going to be able to carry him to bed anymore."

"Here," I say, going to her side. "Let me help." I slide my arms under his little sleeping body and lift him gently so as not to wake him. "Lead the way," I whisper.

Ashlan heads down the hall and into his room, turning on a lamp that shines stars on the ceiling. She pulls back his blankets, and I lay him gingerly on the twin-sized bed. Pulling his blankets back up over him, she takes her time to tuck him in and places a soft kiss on his forehead.

Visions of her doing this in my cabin dance through my head like the sugar plums from the story I just read. Warmth spreads through my body, and I imagine this is what the Grinch felt like when his heart grew in his chest.

She motions for me to follow her into the hallway, where she gently closes his door. "Thank you," she says, smiling up at me.

"Anytime." She doesn't look away, and I find my hands drawn to the sides of her face. I brush my thumbs along her cheeks and watch as her eyes drift closed. She presses her face into my touch. "Let me take you out again, please?"

She nods, and fireworks go off in my chest. "I'd like that."

I feel like I've just won the lottery. "Thank you. You won't regret it."

She stares into my eyes for a moment before smiling softly. "I think you're right."

"Hey," Aiden calls down the hallway. "Are you going to help me unload the truck or stand there making goo-goo eyes at each other all night?"

I shake my head. "Way to ruin a moment," I call back quietly.

Chapter Thirteen

Ashlan

"MOMMY! MOMMY!" EZRA SHOUTS from across the hall. "Santa came!" He comes running into my room holding out his stocking, which Santa left by his bed. "Is it time to go see our presents?"

I grab my cell phone and check the time. "Ezra, it's only five o'clock. Climb in bed with Mommy for a bit and we'll look at your stocking together while we wait for Uncle Aiden and Beau to get here."

"But, Mommy," he whines. "That's gonna be forever!"

I slide up into a sitting position and pat the space next to me. "No, they said they'll be here by six. That's only an hour. Besides, we need to let Grandma rest a little more." Five a.m. is early, even for my mom.

"Okay," he says, scrambling up onto the bed and upending his stocking, dumping the contents out onto my comforter. "Look!"

he says, holding up a Tootsie Roll bank. "Santa gives me this every year." He grins and shakes it. "Can I have one?"

Laughing, I take the bank and put it beside him. "Not yet. You know the rules."

He sighs and then sifts through the rest of the items until he finds a deck of Go Fish cards. "Can we play?" he asks, passing me the box.

"Of course." When Mom comes in at a quarter till six, we're still playing Go Fish, and Ezra's winning.

"Ezra, why don't you take your stocking stuff to your room and let Mommy get dressed?" She winks at me. "Uncle Aiden and Beau will be here any minute."

"Yay!" He gathers all the cards, and I help him slide them back into the box. He puts the rest of his goodies back into the stocking before slipping out the door. My mom follows, but peeks back in before she shuts the door. "Aiden says they're ten minutes out, so you don't have much time to get ready."

"Thanks, Mom."

She grins. "No problem."

By the time Aiden knocks on the door, I'm dressed and my hair and teeth are brushed. Usually, I don't bother changing out of my pajamas until we leave for church, but today feels different.

"Merry Christmas!" Aiden shouts when Ezra comes racing out of his room. "I see Mom's still making you wait in your room in the morning?"

Ezra pouts. "Yeah, she says it's a ta-dition."

Aiden and Mom both laugh. "It's a *tradition*," I say slowly.

"That's what I said." Ezra leans around Aiden's tall frame and finally sees the piles of presents. "Santa *loves* me!" He races into the living room and plops down in front of the tree. "Wow!" His little eyes are huge as saucers as he takes it all in.

"'Wow' is right," Mom says, shaking her head. "You must have been a very good boy this year."

I catch Beau elbowing Aiden in the ribs and laughing. Best uncle ever," Aiden mouths at him.

"Who's going to be Santa's helper?" I ask, looking at Aiden.

"I think Beau should do it," he says, shoving Beau towards the tree.

Beau rubs his hands together and gets down on the floor with Ezra. "Want to help me?"

Ezra grins and nods his head. I watch as they work through the piles, Beau patiently handing presents to Ezra and telling him who to take them to. My heart does a funny flip in my chest, and I can't help but feel like Beau's supposed to be here. With us.

"Go ahead. Open your presents," Mom says once everything's been passed out.

Ezra takes his time opening each present and holding it up for everyone to see. I think it's safe to say this is the best day of his little life. He shoves his hand into a big gift bag and holds up a huge stuffed orange octopus and squeezes it tight.

"Who was that from?" I ask, not remembering buying that one with Aiden.

"I got it for him," Beau says, grinning as Ezra plays with the legs and turns it around in his hands before putting it on his head like a hat.

"Thank you!" Ezra squeals, hugging Beau quickly before going back to his gifts.

Beau's expression goes from happy to stunned. Clearly, he wasn't expecting a hug. He clears his throat and says, "You're welcome."

"Now that he's done, everyone else open your gifts." Mom sits back on the couch, her gifts in a small pile beside her and a huge smile on her face. Christmas is her favorite holiday. After Dad died, we didn't always have a lot, but we had each other, and Christmas was a time she made sure to make us feel special.

I glance at Ezra, happily playing with his new toys, and smile. I only hope I'm doing the same for him.

Beau slides a package out from behind him and passes it to me. "Here, this is for you."

Carefully, I slip my finger under the edge of the wrapping paper and pull. I open the shirt box and reveal a fuzzy, deep purple infinity scarf. The fabric is incredibly soft as I wrap it around my neck. "Thank you so much! It's beautiful."

Beau beams. "Not nearly as beautiful as you," he replies.

"Aww, isn't that sweet," Aiden says, tossing a wad of paper at Beau.

"Here," I say, passing him a small box. "It's not nearly as nice, but . . ."

Beau takes the small box and opens it. "Wow," he says, lifting out the leather wallet. "It's perfect, thank you."

"Wait!" Ezra shouts, jumping up and racing down the hall to his room. A minute later, he's back carrying a stack of papers, glitter floating around him like snow in a snow globe. "I almost forgot." He passes out his projects, grinning as each person tells him how beautiful they are.

"Good luck cleaning the floor," Aiden whispers when Ezra's distracted.

Beau laughs and stands to gather the wrapping paper pieces from the floor. "Get a bag, would you?" he says to Aiden.

After the mess is cleaned up—except for the glitter, which I'm sure we'll be cleaning for the next year—and we eat breakfast, Mom reminds us it's time to get ready for church. "Why don't you two go on ahead and get us seats since you're ready, and Ezra, Aiden and I will be right behind you."

"Sure," Beau says, standing and grabbing his jacket. "Here," he passes me my olive green coat and waits for me to put my boots on before opening the door and guiding me outside.

"Wait," I say, going back inside and grabbing the scarf. "Okay, now I'm ready." I loop the scarf around my neck and follow Beau to his truck.

"I guess it's a good thing you drove today and not Aiden. Otherwise, we'd have to take my car, and I don't think you'd be comfortable."

Beau glances at my little sedan. "I could make it work," he says, winking at me.

Beau's six foot tall, easy. There's no way he'd feel like anything other than a smashed sardine in my car. I resist the urge to giggle at that ridiculous image.

The drive to church is short, and Beau finds a parking space fairly easily. We sit quietly for a moment, watching through the windshield as other parishioners park and file in to church. "You ready for this?" he asks. "Walking into church together? People are going to talk."

I pause with my hand on the door handle. "I didn't even think about it."

He looks away for a moment. "You can go in and I'll come in with your brother, if you want," he suggests. "That way, people won't assume we're together."

Is that what I want? I drop my hands into my lap. "Do you not want people to know we're dating yet?" I ask softly. *That's what we're doing, right?*

He turns in his seat and takes my hands in his. "If I had my way, the whole town would know you're mine. You and Ezra both, but it's fast and I don't want to rush you." He brings my hands to his lips and places a soft kiss on my fingers. "I don't need more dates to know you two are my future. I feel it"—he presses a hand to his heart—"right here."

I suck in a breath, the sincerity in his voice giving me goosebumps. "I don't know what to say."

"You're setting the pace. It's your call." He looks hopeful, but resigned.

"Walk me in?" I ask, before I lose my nerve.

His face lights up brighter than the sun at midday. "You got it."

He opens my door and helps me down from the truck, closes the door and links his fingers in mine, then leads the way into church. I can see when people notice us holding hands and start whispering to one another, but I just smile, and keep walking until Beau stops by a mostly empty pew. "How's this?" he asks.

"Perfect," I say, removing my coat and laying it out to save seats for everyone else.

He shifts uncomfortably in his seat a few times before finally reaching out and holding my hand in his. "Sorry," he whispers. "I forgot how many people come to Christmas service."

I rub my thumb along the top of his hand, relishing the warmth of his fingers between mine. "Not a fan of crowds?" I ask, remembering he seemed uncomfortable at his parents' funeral as well, but I chalked that up to the situation.

He shakes his head. "No, I'm not. I didn't realize how much I disliked them until we lived in Austin. It's part of the reason I wanted to move back home and up the mountain."

"Hey," Mom says, guiding Ezra to sit next to me. "Thanks for the seats."

"Can I sit by you?" Ezra asks Beau.

"Sure." Beau ruffles his hair and pulls him into the space between us. I scoot over to make a little more room.

"They look cozy," I hear a voice behind me say. "It's about time someone realized what a catch she is."

My face blooms with heat, and I clear my throat to let them know we can hear them. Beau reaches an arm out behind Ezra and places it on my shoulder. He leans to me and whispers, "They're right, you know. You two are a catch."

Chapter Fourteen

Beau

"YOU'RE GOING INTO TOWN again?" Aiden asks a few weeks later. "I thought you moved up here to avoid town."

I shrug into a light jacket and grab my wallet and keys from the makeshift plywood counter. "I have to go pick out the countertops today."

He laughs. "Uh huh. Tell Ashlan I said hi."

"Will do," I say, walking out the door. The last few weeks have been a blur of cabin renovations, and finding excuses to head into town to have lunch with Ash. The inside is nearly complete now. I've redone the bathroom and put up new cabinets. All that's left is new counters, then I can start on the outside as soon as the weather warms up.

Thirty minutes later, I'm walking into the Coffee Loft to get Ashlan for lunch. These lunch dates are the highlight of my days.

"You ready?" I ask, leaning against the wall while she clocks out and grabs her things.

"Yep!" She says something to Ember and heads my way. "Where to?"

I check the time. "Beats and Eats will have to do. I have a meeting in Barberville in a little bit. That okay?"

She nods and follows me out to the sidewalk. "Sounds good. Mind if we walk?"

I hit the button to make sure my truck is locked and lace my fingers through hers. "Not at all."

She seems lost in thought today, and I can't help but wonder what's going on in her head. "You okay?"

She leans her head against my shoulder, and I can't resist placing a kiss on the top of her head. "Yeah. Just thinking."

"Want to share?" I ask, leading her across the road to the diner.

"Let's sit down first."

Suddenly, I'm not so sure I want to hear what she's thinking after all. Is this the part where she breaks up with me? "After you," I say, holding open the door.

"Hey, y'all," Patty, one of the servers, says. "Take a seat anywhere."

I nod and guide Ashlan to a booth in the back.

"Know what you're going to get?"

She smiles. "I always get the same thing."

Chuckling, I grab a menu from the box on the table. "I think I might try something different today."

"Brave," she says.

"Hey, sorry about that. What can I get y'all to drink?" Patty asks, coming by our table.

"Water, please," Ashlan says.

"Me too, please."

"Y'all ready to order?" Patty asks, pulling out her notepad.

Ashlan looks at me and I motion for her to go first. "I'll have the fried chicken plate with green beans and mashed potatoes."

Patty scribbles it onto her pad and looks to me. "And for you?"

"Same," I say, grinning and sliding the menu back in place at the end of the table.

"Great, I'll get this out as soon as it's ready." Patty slips the notebook back in her apron and walks away, stopping at a nearby table and chatting for a moment.

"So . . ." I say, hoping Ashlan will start talking now that we've ordered.

"Well"—she clears her throat—"Aurora's pregnant, as you know, and due to have that little munchkin next month."

I nod. "Will she be taking some time off after the baby is born?"

Patty stops by and places our water on the table before moving along to help another table.

"That's just it," she says. "She's thinking of not coming back after the baby is born."

"Like closing the Coffee Loft, or . . ." I could see why that would worry Ashlan. She loves her job.

She shakes her head. "No, not closing it, just not working anymore. At least, not day-to-day stuff."

"Okay," I say, relieved she's not facing losing a job she loves. "So, what's got you so lost in thought?"

"She wants to promote me to manager. It's more money, and more responsibility. I'd be working more hours. What if I can't be there for Ezra the way I'd like?"

I reach out and take her hands in mine. "I'm sure it would work out. If you wanted to take the position, your mom would certainly help with Ezra. I would, too."

She nods. "I told Aurora I would consider it, but I need to decide soon so she can interview for the position if I turn it down."

"You have some time. Think it over. For what it's worth, I think you'd do a great job managing the Coffee Loft. You love that place."

She grins. "I really do. What's not to love about being surrounded by coffee all day?"

I can think of a few things "not to love," but I let it go.

"Here we go," Patty says, placing our meals on the table. "Let me know if you need anything else."

We change the subject and talk about the weather and the cabin renovations while we eat.

"Excuse me," Ashlan says, sliding out of the booth. "I'll be right back." She walks past me into the bathrooms just as my phone rings in my pocket.

Glancing at the caller ID, I see it's Landon, a friend and fellow software developer from Austin.

"Hello?"

"Hey, Beau. How've you been?"

"Good," I say, pushing my plate away. "What's up? I haven't heard from you in months."

Landon laughs. "Always straight to the point, my man. Listen, I need your help. We have a project that we are way behind on, and I think you could get us back on track."

Excitement hums in my veins. Last I heard, they were working on a big superhero game. "You know I don't live in Austin anymore, right?"

Landon sighs. "I know. The thing is, we really need your help, so if you could come out for a few days to get a feel for the project and pick up some hardware, I've gotten the higher ups to agree to let you work remotely."

"When would you need me?" I ask, mentally going over my schedule.

"As soon as you could make it."

I think about it for a minute. The cabin's coming to a place where the things I can do on my own are done. I need to hire out most everything else on the list. Which means, I'll have more time on my hands. "Sure," I say. "I can be there next week. I just need to wrap some things up here, first."

"Thanks, man. You're a lifesaver."

"You bet, but you owe me dinner. You know I hadn't planned on coming back to Austin." I mean it, too. If I couldn't work remotely on this project, I'd have turned it down. No matter how exciting the project might be.

Landon laughs. "You got it. See ya next week. I'll have my secretary handle flights and email you the details."

"Sounds good, man. Talk to you later." I hang up and grin. I hadn't really considered contracting, but it makes sense. I can do what I love and stay here in Piney Brook with the people I love.

"I have to get back," Ashlan says, grabbing her bag and avoiding my gaze. "Sorry."

"Okay, if you give me a second, I can pay the bill and walk you back."

She shakes her head. "No, it's okay. Ember called and says she needs me back right away. I'll just see you later."

"Okay." I stand and pull her in for a hug. "I'll call you later?"

She nods her head and turns to walk out. Something feels off, but I can't place my finger on it. Hopefully, I'll get her to talk to me later.

🐾　🐾　🐾　🐾　🐾

I spent way too long at the countertop distributor looking at different types of materials and patterns, and I'm exhausted. I pull into the driveway and sigh, relieved that I'm finally home for the evening.

Aiden comes stomping out the front door and yanks open my car door. "Dude, are you serious?" I ask.

"Are you?" He's fuming. "I just came from Mom's, where Ash is moping around like someone kicked her puppy. Her eyes are all red like she's been crying, but she won't talk about it. Which leads me to believe you did something that has her worked up."

"What?" I ask, confused. "I knew she was upset, but I didn't think she was that upset."

He shakes his head. "You knew she was upset, and you just left her like that?"

I throw my hands in the air. "It was just about work. What was I supposed to do?" I ask. "She said she needed to think about it some more."

He shakes his head. "You're lucky I don't punch you in the face for making my baby sister cry." He walks over to his truck, climbs inside, and drives away.

What just happened?

Chapter Fifteen

Ashlan

I BARELY MAKE IT out of Beats and Eats before the tears start to fall. He's leaving. Again. And here I thought we were in a really good place. Stupid me letting myself fall in love with him.

"Are you okay?" Ember asks when I step back inside the Coffee Loft.

Shaking my head, I walk right into the restrooms to wash my face. I have a job to do. I can fall apart later.

By the time my shift ends, I've gone from upset to mad to upset again. If he had plans to leave and go back to Austin, why even ask me out?

Clocking out, I wave goodbye to Ember and remind her to call me if there's a problem. Aurora and Bradley are away on a babymoon and I don't want to bother them unless we have to.

"You got it," she says. "I hope your day gets better."

I grimace. "Me too," I say.

Twenty minutes later, I'm pulling into the driveway and sigh. Of course, Aiden would be here tonight. I flip down the visor and open the mirror practicing schooling my face so I don't lose it. One of the things I worried about was putting Aiden in the middle. I can't do that to Beau. He may have broken my heart, but my brother's all he has left.

"Mommy!" Ezra yells, running to me as soon as I open the door. He throws his little arms around my middle and squeezes.

"Did you have a good day?" I ask, fighting tears. It's not just me that will be affected when Beau leaves. Ezra's fallen for him just as much as I have. A second man who will walk right out of his life. I tilt my head back and will the tears to go away.

"I did! Mrs. Morgan let me read a book to the class 'bout sharks. I only needed a little help, too."

"Wow," my brother says, coming into the living room. "I didn't know you could read."

I force a smile. "They've been learning sight words all year. He's actually getting pretty good."

Aiden studies my face, and I shake my head. "Ezra, why don't you go see if Grandma needs help setting the table."

"Okay," he says, padding off to the kitchen where I can hear Mom taking something out of the oven.

"What's wrong?" Aiden asks once Ezra's out of ear shot.

"Nothing," I lie. I turn and kick my shoes off. "I'm going to go change before dinner."

Aiden steps in front of me. "Ashlan, what happened?"

I groan. "You're a real pain, you know that?" I step around him and resist the urge to speed walk down the hall.

Closing my bedroom door behind me, I sink onto my bed and let the tears fall for the second time today. I've been so consumed by my own feelings, I haven't even considered Ezra's. What kind of mother does that make me?

A knock at my door has me wiping my eyes. "Ash, you okay?" Mom asks.

"Yep," I say, shucking my jeans and Coffee Loft polo. "Just changing. I'll be out in a sec."

"Aiden said you look upset."

I roll my eyes. "Aiden's crazy. I'm fine." Aiden needs to mind his own business.

"Okay. Well, dinner's almost ready."

"Sounds good." I grab a pair of leggings and an oversized shirt and slip them on. Once I'm sure Mom's not standing by my door, I open it and make a beeline for the bathroom. I take my time splashing cold water on my face and washing my hands before heading to the dining room.

"Where's Beau?" Ezra asks when I finally sit down.

"He had things to do today," I say, giving him a smile. He may be leaving, but he's still Aiden's best friend, and I don't want Ezra to think badly of him when I know he'll still be around from time to time.

Aiden watches my every move like a hawk. "Aiden, please. I know I'm prettier than you, but you can stop staring." Deflect. That should work.

He scoffs. "I'm not pretty. I'm handsome. Right, E?"

Ezra giggles. "I think you're pretty and handsome."

Aiden shakes his head and laughs. "Thanks, little man."

"So," Mom says, eyeing me from across the table. "How was work?"

I fill my plate. Mom's meatloaf is usually my favorite, but tonight, I have no appetite. This hurts worse than when TJ refused to believe he was Ezra's father. "It was good. Aurora let me know she's decided not to come back after the baby's born." I push my food around my plate.

"Is that what's got you so upset?" Aiden asks, a look of confusion on his face. "Is she closing the store or something?"

I shake my head. "No, she's actually offering me the management position. She's keeping the Coffee Loft. She just doesn't want to have to be there every day."

"Oh, that's wonderful," Mom says, beaming. "You've really enjoyed being the assistant manager. I'm sure you'd love to run the store for her."

I nod. "It means more hours, and more time away, though." I glance at Ezra. "I'm not sure I'm ready to commit to that much time."

Mom follows my gaze. "I think it is a wonderful opportunity, but it's up to you."

Aiden shrugs. "Would you make enough to move out?"

Mom slaps his arm. "Aiden Dewitt. Ashlan and Ezra can stay here as long as they like, regardless of how much she makes."

Aiden rubs his arm. "Obviously. I just figured she might be ready for a place of her own." He goes back to eating and drops it, thankfully.

"You know I'll always help you with Ezra. And, I'm sure Beau would help, too," Mom says.

At the sound of Beau's name, I flinch.

Aiden freezes and growls, "What did he do?"

"I have no idea what you're talking about," I say, shoveling a huge bite of meatloaf into my mouth.

Aiden narrows his eyes and watches me. "If you say so."

By the time Aiden leaves, I'm exhausted, and I still need to get Ezra in bed. "Come on," I say, picking him up and heading to his room. "Let's get you tucked in, shall we?"

"Aww, Mom. It's too early for bed." He leans his head on my shoulder. "Can you read to me, at least?"

"How about we let Mommy get some sleep, and I'll read to you tonight?" Mom says, coming up and reaching out for him.

"Okay." He leans in and gives me a kiss on the cheek. "Night night, Mommy. Don't let the bedbugs bite."

I tickle his little sides as I hand him over to Mom. "Night, night, Ezra. See you in the morning." I mouth "thank you" to Mom, then slip into my room and fall into bed.

My phone shows a missed call from Beau, but I turn it off and roll over. I can't talk to him tonight. I can't hear him tell me he's leaving. Not yet.

⬚ ⬚ ⬚ ⬚ ⬚

Aiden's sitting at the table when I head into the kitchen in the morning to get a cup of coffee. "What are you doing here?" I ask. "I thought the wifi was working at the cabin."

Aiden stares at me and shakes his head. "It is. I just couldn't stay there last night."

Dread sits heavy in my gut. "What did you do?" I ask.

He shakes his head. "Nothing. He's lucky, too."

"Aiden," I say, frustration lacing my tone. "Beau didn't do anything wrong." Well, not technically.

"He knew you were upset, and didn't do anything about it. That's something wrong, in my book."

I shake my head. "I didn't give him a chance. I overheard him on the phone and left before he could tell me he is moving back to Austin."

"Wait, what?" His nose wrinkles. "Beau's not moving back to Austin."

I nod. "Yeah, he is. I heard him on the phone. He leaves next week."

Aiden frowns. "I really think you must have heard wrong."

"I wish," I mutter. "I have to get ready for work and get Ezra to school. Can we talk about this later?"

Aiden nods. "Sure."

The rest of the morning passes in a blur, and I walk into the Coffee Loft just in time to open. The steady stream of morning customers keeps my mind busy and off of the impending conversation I know I'll have to have with Beau.

At ten o'clock, Ember comes in and takes over behind the counter. I quickly clean the dining room, and head to the back to grab what we need to restock after the morning rush. "Here," I say, pushing through the door to the front, arms loaded down with bags of coffee and jugs of cream. "Help me with this, would you?"

"Here," a deep voice says, stepping up and grabbing the items from my overfull hands.

"Beau," I whisper. Clearing my throat, I try again. "Thanks, but what are you doing here?"

Beau sets the haul onto the counter and nods at Ember. "You okay if we step outside and talk for a second?"

Ember grins and nods her head. "I've got it."

Beau places his hand on my lower back and gently guides me outside. "I think we should talk."

Chapter Sixteen

Beau

When Aiden called this morning to ask if I was moving back to Austin, I realized Ash had overheard my conversation with Landon and jumped to the wrong conclusion. I debated waiting until she was off work to talk to her, but I can't wait that long.

"I'm working, Beau," she says, as I lead her to a bench just down the sidewalk from the entrance where we can have a bit of privacy.

"I know. I'll make it quick," I say. Hoping that once she hears what I have to say, she'll understand I'm in this for the long haul. "I think you overheard my conversation yesterday, and I wanted to clear some things up."

She sniffles. "It's fine. I understand. It's not like we made any promises to each other or anything."

I shake my head and stand. "Ashlan, you don't understand."

She looks up at me, her bottom lip trembling. "Just do me a favor," she says. "Keep in touch with Ezra, he doesn't deserve to lose another man from his life."

I drop to my knees in front of her. "Ashlan, baby, I'm not going anywhere. I mean, I am, but not permanently. I have to fly out to Austin for a few days next week to come up to speed on a project, then I'll be back here and working remotely."

Her watery eyes search mine. "What?"

"Landon, a guy I know from the tech industry in Austin, reached out and offered me a remote position contracting on a project he's leading."

"Remote?" she asks.

I nod. "Yes. Remote. I'm not leaving Piney Brook. I can't. It's where my heart is."

She drops her head in her hands. "I'm so sorry," she whispers. "I heard you were leaving and I panicked."

Gently, I tilt her face up where she can see me. "Ashlan, I'm not going anywhere. Not now, not ever. This is my home. You and Ezra are my home. So, unless you tell me you want to move, this is where we will stay."

She searches my eyes for a moment and must see how serious I am because she throws her arms around my neck and hugs me tight. "I love you," she says into my shoulder.

My heart soars. I've dreamed of hearing those words from her, but the reality is so much better than anything I could have ever imagined. "I love you, too," I say, standing and pulling her up with me. "I'm going to kiss you now, is that okay?"

She wipes tears away from her cheeks. "Yes, please," she breathes.

Aware of being on the street where anyone can see, I gently press my lips to hers before pulling away and putting some distance between us.

"Are we good?" I ask, wanting to make sure before I walk her back into the Coffee Loft.

"We're good," she says, hugging her arms around my middle again.

I kiss her forehead when I walk her back into work, reluctant to leave her. "I'll call you tonight."

She grins and walks back inside. "I'm counting on it."

🪴 🪴 🪴 🪴 🪴

"You guys heading to Blue Zoo today?" Aiden asks, packing the rest of his things in his duffle bag. He's heading back to his place in Austin today, and he's been cleaning out his room since breakfast.

"We are." It's been two weeks since the mishap with the phone call. The trip to Austin was short, and it was nice seeing everyone, but I'm glad to be back home.

He nods. "Good, Ezra will love that." He zips the bag and slings it over his shoulder. "I have to say, the cabin looks pretty good these days."

I look around and smile, a sense of satisfaction washing over me. New marble countertops sit atop gray Shaker-style cabinets. The walls are stained a light gray, making the space look much more open and inviting than when I purchased it. "Thanks, and thanks for all your help. I wouldn't have gotten this far without you."

Aiden laughs. "I'm glad you hired a company to replace the plumbing and the windows. That's way beyond my pay grade."

"I know my limits," I say, running my hand along the new counter tops. "Besides, with this new job, I needed to free up some time."

Aiden shoots me a look. "I was sure you'd take a year off."

I chuckle. "Me too, honestly, but this deal was too good to pass up."

"Good thing the internet's working now." He laughs and slings his bag over his shoulder. "Well, I better get going. It's a long drive back to Austin." He steps over and gives me a brotherly hug. "Take care of my sister and nephew, would ya?"

"Yep." I say, happy that he's not still angry about the misunderstanding. "That's the plan."

"Speaking of plans," he says. "Don't forget to ask my permission before you pop the question."

I shake my head. "You're crazy. I'd ask your mom, not you."

Aiden laughs. "Fair enough, but just so you know, I'd say yes."

He turns on his heel and heads out the front door. "See ya," he calls before closing the door behind him.

It's only been a little over a month since we started dating, way too soon to pop the question, but it's good to know Aiden approves. I glance at my watch. Time to go.

The moment we step into the aquarium, Ezra's eyes widen like saucers—he's practically vibrating with excitement. I can't help but grin as he pulls me toward the first exhibit, a massive tank teeming with colorful fish darting around like they're in some underwater dance-off.

"Beau! Look at that one!" Ezra shouts, pointing at a clownfish. "It looks just like Nemo!" His voice is filled with pure joy, and his excitement is contagious.

"That's cool, buddy!" I say, crouching down to his level. "Do you see the anemone?" I ask, pointing to the flowerlike sea creature.

"It looks like it has fingers," he giggles.

Ashlan laughs from behind us. "It kind of does, but you know what I was really hoping we might see today?"

Ezra shakes his head. "What?"

"An octopus," she says, winking at me.

"Octopus!" he echoes, his face lighting up. "Can we see them now?"

"Absolutely. Let's find them." I take his small hand in mine, and he practically bounces on his toes as we walk together towards the octopus exhibit. He's been sleeping every night with the stuffed octopus I got him for Christmas. When Ashlan shared that with me, I felt like the king of the universe. Aiden may have purchased the toy store, but I'm the one who gave him the gift he sleeps with.

As we approach the octopus exhibit, I reach out for Ashlan's hand. She's smiling, a relaxed look on her face that makes my heart skip a beat. I love spending time with them like this when we are all carefree and not worried about homework or adult responsibilities. Just the three of us, together, making memories.

"Look! There's the octopus!" Ezra squeals, pointing at the large tank, where the large bulbous creature is swimming, its tentacles flowing like ribbons through the water. "Wow," Ezra gasps. "It's big!" He leans over the railing, squirming in place.

Just then, a friendly aquarium worker approaches, wearing a light blue polo shirt with neon green accents. "Hello, there! Do you like octopuses?" she asks, kneeling down to meet Ezra's eye level.

"Yes," Ezra says shyly.

"It's his favorite," Ashlan adds.

"Inky here is my favorite, too," the worker says. "He's a master of disguise. Did you know octopuses can change their colors to blend in with their surroundings?"

Ezra nods. "It's camouflage," he says, warming up to the newcomer.

"That's right," she says. "My name is Amber. What's your name?"

"Ezra."

"Nice to meet you, Ezra. What else do you know about octopuses?"

He shrugs. "I know they can fit in small places."

She nods, her eyes twinkling with delight. "You're right. They're super smart too. Did you know they can open jars to get their food?"

Ezra shakes his head. "Can we see him do that?" he asks excitedly.

"It's not time for him to eat right now, but I can show you a video if it's okay with your mom and dad." She lifts the iPad hanging from her shoulder. "It's an educational video from our aquarium."

Ezra spins and pokes his bottom lip out. "Please?" he asks.

"It's fine with me," Ashlan says, stepping closer to me and squeezing my hand.

It seems more and more people are making the assumption I'm Ezra's dad. At first, it startled me, but now . . . it feels right. I'd be lucky for him to consider me his dad someday.

After showing Ezra the video—twice—Amber gives him an octopus sticker. "I have to go back to work now, but if you watch closely, you might get to see him change colors or even squirt some water." She gestures to Inky who's changing color from a muted brown to a vibrant red in his tank.

"Whoa! Do you see that?" Ezra asks, pulling on my hand.

"I do. Looks like Inky wanted to show you his cool tricks." I glance up and catch Ashlan's reflection in the glass. She's watching us, a peaceful smile on her face.

"All right," Ashlan says, coming to stand closer to us. "I think we have some more exploring to do."

Ezra looks torn. "We can visit Inky again on our way out," I offer. "Then, I was thinking we should have chicken nuggets and ice cream after? How does that sound?"

"Great!" Ezra shouts, and I can't help but think that today, surrounded by wonder and excitement, everything feels just right.

⁂

"Thank you," Ashlan says in the car on the way home. "I think it's safe to say he had a great day."

I glance in the rearview mirror and see Ezra fast asleep in his booster seat, his arms wrapped around a stuffed replica of Inky. "I'm glad, so did I."

"I was thinking . . ." she says, hesitating.

"Go ahead," I say reassuringly. "You can tell me anything."

She glances back at her sleeping son, a soft smile tugging at her lips. "Well, I was wondering if you'd be my Valentine's Day date to the annual hospital fundraiser."

"I'd love to," I say, reaching over and squeezing her hand. "I've never been. Is it fancy?" I haven't worn a suit in months, but I'm sure the one I have stuck in the back of the closet still fits.

"It's a suit and tie type of affair."

"No problem," I say, winking at her. "I can handle that."

"Great," she says, sounding relieved.

"I'm not sure there's anything you could ask me that I'd say no to, Ashlan." She's got me, hook, line and sinker, and I wouldn't trade it for the world.

Ezra sleeps the entire way back to their house, and I can't help but sneak glances at him in the rearview. He's so rarely still.

I pull into the driveway and put the truck in park. "I'll help you get him inside," I say, stepping down from the cab and heading around to the other side. Thankfully, I'd purchased the truck with an extended cab. I may have needed to drive people around in Austin, but I couldn't give up having a truck. It's too much a part of who I am.

After taking Ezra inside and laying him in his bed, I meet Ashlan in the living room.

"Are you sure you need to go?" she asks. "I could make some hot chocolate and we could just talk."

I pull her to me and place a light kiss on her forehead. "I've got some work to finish up for this contract I'm on, but I'd love to take you to dinner Friday night if you're free?"

She nods, leaning in for a hug. "That sounds perfect."

I linger, holding her in my arms a bit longer, before stepping back and moving toward the front door.

"Hey, Beau?" Ashlan calls.

"Yeah?"

"Are you going to kiss me goodbye?"

My mouth falls open, and for a moment, I can't believe what I just heard. I've been holding back for weeks, taking things slow, waiting for her to set the pace. Other than our first kiss outside the Coffee Loft, that still runs through my mind, I've kept it to short pecks—barely. But now? The invitation hangs in the air, giving me permission to finally kiss her like I've dreamed about.

"I would love to," I choke out, my voice rougher than I intended. She's standing there in the middle of the living room, her cheeks tinged with the faintest blush, looking so beautiful it almost hurts.

I close the space between us in three long strides, unable to hold back anymore. My hands cup her face, her skin soft and warm beneath my palms. "I've been dying to kiss you again," I confess, my voice a low growl. The words aren't enough to convey just how much I've wanted this, but it's all I have before my lips crash against hers.

She sighs softly and wraps her arms around my neck. Her fingers thread through my hair and pull me closer causing a shiver to race down my spine. I step closer and erase the sliver of space left between us. Her body melts into mine. The world could end right now, and I wouldn't care. This isn't just a kiss—it's an explosion. Like a bomb has gone off releasing every feeling I've buried for too long. If this isn't heaven, I don't want to know what is.

Chapter Seventeen

Ashlan

I STAND IN FRONT of my bedroom mirror, nervously smoothing down my red wrap dress. The soft fabric clings to my curves in all the right places, but I can't help second-guessing my choice. Is it too much for a dinner date with your son tagging along? We'd decided to forgo the Valentine's ball and have a family dinner instead, and I can't say I'm disappointed.

"Mom, have you seen my Inky?" Ezra's voice carries from down the hall.

"Check under your bed, bud," I call back, checking my reflection for the hundredth time.

I run my fingers through my dark hair, debating whether to leave it down or pin it up. Down, I finally decide. Beau seems to like it down, though he's never said so outright.

My stomach does a little flip at the thought of him. Things have been going so well, and I can't help daydreaming about becoming Mrs. Beau Travers one day.

"You look beautiful, honey," Mom says, appearing in the doorway. "Happiness looks good on you."

I feel a blush creeping up my cheeks. "Thanks, Mom."

The doorbell chimes, and Ezra's feet slap on the tile as he runs down the hall to open the door. "Ezra, wait for me," Mom calls, following him down the hall.

I hear the front door open and Ezra giggle. Smiling, I pick up my purse, slip on my shoes, and head to the living room to my boys. When did I start thinking that way?

I round the corner, and there stands Beau, looking dashing in a dark green button-down and dark jeans. My heart does a little flip.

"You look gorgeous," he says with that smile that never fails to make me melt. He passes me a huge bouquet of red roses, just like our first date. "These are for you."

I bring them to my nose and inhale their sweet scent. "Thank you."

Ezra tugs on Beau's arm, and he crouches down to meet Ezra at eye level. "Are you ready for our big night out?"

Ezra nods vigorously, his dark hair flopping with the movement. "I'm gonna get the biggest burger ever!"

I can't help but laugh. "We'll see about that. Don't forget your jacket."

"Beau says we can eat the biggest burgers we want," he says, scooting closer to Beau. "Right?"

Beau laughs. "You bet. As long as it's okay with Mom."

Ezra frowns. "Aw, man. She always makes me order a kid's meal. Those are for babies."

Beau and I can't help but laugh as Ezra slips his shoes on the wrong feet. I pass the flowers to Mom, who's waiting to see us off. "Come on," I say, helping him right his shoes. "We'll talk about your burger when we get there."

As we pile into Beau's truck, I catch a whiff of his cologne—a woodsy scent that reminds me of pine trees and cozy campfires. Ezra chatters away in the backseat, trying to convince me he needs a big burger because he's a big kid now. Oh, to be five.

The new burger place is bustling when we arrive. The warm glow of string lights and the aroma of grilled meat welcome us at the door. Beau steps up to the counter, lifting Ezra on his hip. "I was thinking we should order a smaller burger and a milkshake. It wouldn't do to have your tummy too full for a shake, right?"

"Yeah!" Ezra says, pumping his little fist in the air. "That sounds good, right Mom?"

"Sounds good to me," I say, laughing at his excitement. "It is a special occasion, after all."

We place our order and wait off to the side. When they call our number, Beau grabs our tray of food and nods to the back patio. "Why don't we sit outside tonight, then you can play on the slides when you're done?"

Ezra grabs my hand and leads the way to an empty table right next to the play set. Beau sets our food out, and I help Ezra open his burger wrapper before sitting down next to him and opening my own. I glance up and freeze. Sitting at a nearby table is a face I'd hoped never to see again. TJ.

My stomach knots up, and I instinctively pull Ezra closer to me. "Actually," I say, my voice barely above a whisper, "could we maybe sit somewhere else?" The last thing I want is for TJ to start drama in front of Ezra. But it's too late. TJ's gaze meets mine, then flicks to Ezra. His eyes widen slightly, and I feel my heart rate skyrocket.

"Mommy, what's wrong?" Ezra asks, tugging at my hand. "Your face looks funny."

Beau catches my gaze and turns to see what has me so spooked. Muttering a curse, he turns and grins big. "Ezra, I have a joke for you," he says. "How do you make an octopus laugh?"

Ezra giggles. "I don't know."

"With ten-tickles. Get it?" Beau says, laughing when Ezra finally gets the joke.

"Let's eat," I say, forcing a smile, and trying to keep my voice steady. "This food looks delicious."

As we eat, I can feel TJ's eyes on us. Beau, ever perceptive, leans in close. "Everything will be fine," he murmurs. "Just ignore him."

I nod, not trusting my voice just yet. Ezra, oblivious to the tension, eagerly digs in, using his french fries to scoop ketchup out of the little container Beau supplied him.

Ezra tries telling Beau a joke, and messes up the punch line terribly, but Beau laughs along like it was the greatest joke he's ever heard. As I watch them interact, a warmth spreads through my chest, momentarily pushing away the anxiety of TJ's presence. This, I remind myself, is what matters. This little family we're building, one dinner date at a time.

Ezra runs off to play on the playground, and I'm just starting to relax when I feel a tap on my shoulder. My heart sinks as I turn to see TJ standing there, his face a mask of discomfort.

"Ashlan," he says, his voice low. "Can we talk for a minute?"

I glance at Beau, who gives me a reassuring nod. "I've got this," he mouths, turning his attention back to Ezra. "If you need me, I'll be right here," he says louder, giving TJ a meaningful look.

Reluctantly, I slide out of the chair and follow TJ to a quiet corner of the restaurant. The cheerful chatter of other patrons around us feels surreal against the tension thrumming through my body.

"Look," TJ starts, running a hand through his hair. "I couldn't help but notice . . . he looks just like me."

I swallow hard, my throat suddenly dry. "Yes, he does." Luckily, that's the only way they're alike. Why is he even speaking to me?

TJ's eyes dart back to our table, then back to me. "I need you to understand something. I can't . . . I don't want any part of this. Of him."

His words hit me like a physical blow, and I struggle to keep my composure. A wave of nausea rolls over me. "You made that perfectly clear years ago, TJ. I've never asked anything of you, and that's not going to change. What makes you think I would want you in our lives?" I manage to say, my voice barely above a whisper.

"Just . . . keep him away from me, okay?" TJ's face is a mixture of guilt and determination. "I've got my own life now, and I can't have this complicating things."

For years, I have played nice, hoping to leave the door open for a relationship between them if Ezra decides he wants one. Tonight, something inside me snaps and I can't hold back anymore. My hands ball into fists at my sides. I want to either slap him or laugh in his face, but I don't want to give him that much of my energy. "You don't need to worry about that. I have no intention of exposing my son to the likes of you."

TJ steps back, eyebrows raised in shock at my outburst, then turns and leaves. As he walks away, I take a deep breath, plastering on a smile before returning to our table. Ezra looks up at me, his blue eyes sparkling. "Mommy, look what I can do!" He runs off toward the rock wall and starts climbing.

"Wow," I call out. "You're so strong!" I slide into my chair beside Beau and sigh. That could have been worse. I feel sorry for anyone who doesn't want to know this amazing son of mine.

Beau's warm hand finds mine under the table, giving it a gentle squeeze. I meet his concerned gaze and manage a small smile.

"Want to tell me what happened back there?" Beau asks softly, his deep brown eyes filled with concern.

I take a shaky breath, the emotions I've been holding back threatening to spill over. "He... he was surprised Ezra looked so much like him. He made it clear he wants nothing to do with us. That he doesn't want the 'complications.'"

Beau's jaw tightens, but his voice remains gentle. "I'm sorry."

"It's just . . ." I pause, watching Ezra pump his legs on the swing, his face alight with joy. "I feel terrible that Ezra hasn't grown up with a dad. He deserves all those things that only a dad can give. The times I spent with my dad growing up were some of the best of my life."

Beau shifts beside me, taking both of my hands in his. His touch is warm, grounding. "Ashlan, look at me," he says, his voice low and earnest. "Ezra does have a dad. Me. And I'm not going anywhere."

My breath catches in my throat, and I search Beau's face, hardly daring to believe what I'm hearing. "Beau, I . . . you don't have to be his dad to be an important person in his life."

Beau's lips curve into that gentle smile. "I know that," he says, wrapping his arm around my shoulders. "I love Ezra as if he were my own. And I love you, Ashlan. The three of us . . . we're a family."

Tears prick at my eyes, but for the first time tonight, they're tears of joy and relief. I lean into Beau's solid warmth, watching as Ezra waves to us from the top of the slide. "We love you too, Beau," I whisper, feeling a weight lift from my shoulders. "More than you know."

Epilogue

THE WARM SAND SIFTS between my toes as I walk along the shoreline, the gentle rhythm of the waves creating a peaceful vibe, even though the beach is packed with families. I can't help but smile as I watch Ashlan and Ezra splashing in the shallow water, laughing and giggling when a wave comes and laps at their legs.

"Beau! Come join us!" Ashlan calls, waving me over.

I chuckle, shaking my head. "I'm good here, thanks! Someone has to keep an eye on our stuff!"

Truthfully, I'm content to observe from a distance, savoring this moment of pure joy between mother and son. It's been a whirlwind since I surprised them with this beach trip. I'm not good at keeping secrets, but the look on their faces when I presented the tickets was priceless.

Ezra comes running up to me, kicking up sand in his wake. His hair's slick with seawater, and a huge grin is plastered across his face. "This is the best surprise ever, Beau!"

I ruffle his hair, laughing. "I'm glad you're having fun. Did you see any sharks out there?"

Ezra shakes his head. "No, not yet. I'll keep looking."

Ashlan laughs. "Hopefully we won't see any sharks in the water." She shudders. "I don't want to be lunch."

Ezra giggles. "Mommy, sharks don't like to eat humans. We taste yucky. Like broccoli."

Ashlan grabs a beach towel and dries off. When she slipped out of her cover-up and revealed the light blue swimsuit beneath, my mouth went dryer than the Sahara. She's stunning, and she's mine. Well, if all goes as planned, anyway.

She spreads out the towel on one of the beach chairs I rented and lays back. "I'm going to read for a bit."

Ezra tugs at my hand. "Can you search for shells with me?"

My heart swells. I love spending time with Ezra. "You bet."

We search the shore for a while before heading back and sitting with our toes in the water. "What has been your favorite part of the trip so far?" I ask.

Ezra throws his arms open wide. "Everything!"

I laugh and ruffle his salty hair. "I'm glad."

"What are you two up to?" Ashlan asks, joining us at the water's edge.

"Oh, you know," I reply, "just plotting world domination. The usual."

Ezra giggles and nods his head. "The usual."

She rolls her eyes, but I can see the smile tugging at her lips. "Well, if you two masterminds are done, how about we grab some ice cream?"

Ezra's eyes light up. "Yes! Can I get two scoops?"

I exchange a glance with Ashlan, and we both nod. "I think we can make that happen," I say, already anticipating the sugar rush that's sure to follow.

As we make our way up the beach, I can't help but feel a sense of contentment wash over me. This—right here, right now—is everything. And I wouldn't trade it for the world.

*　*　*　*　*

The next morning, Ezra and I head out for a walk on the beach, letting Ashlan sleep in. He'd stayed the night in my room last night so that we wouldn't disturb her this morning. I take a deep breath, savoring the salty air and the warmth of the sun on my skin. Ezra's small hand is in mine as we walk along the shoreline, his eyes scanning the beach for cool shells. I can't help but smile, realizing how much this little guy has wormed his way into my heart.

"Hey, Ezra," I say, my voice a bit shakier than I'd like. "Can I ask you something important?"

He looks up at me and grins. "Sure! Is it about sharks? Because I know lots about sharks now. Mrs. Morgan let me read lots of books about them."

I chuckle, shaking my head. "Not about sharks this time, buddy. It's about your mom."

Ezra's brow furrows adorably. "Okay, but she's probably still sleeping."

I chuckle. "Actually, I was wondering . . . how would you feel if I asked your mom to marry me?"

Ezra stops in his tracks, his mouth forming a perfect "O." For a moment, my heart stops. I'm worried I've overstepped. But then his face breaks into the biggest grin I've ever seen.

"Really?" he squeals, bouncing on his toes. "You want to be my dad?"

I nod, emotion thick in my throat. "I'd love to be your dad, Ezra. If that's okay with you."

"Okay!" he laughs, throwing his arms around my waist. "Can we tell Mom right now? When do we get married?"

"Whoa, slow down there, buddy," I laugh, ruffling his hair. "We need to ask your mom first. Think she'll say yes?"

Ezra nods vigorously. "She likes you a whole bunch. She gets all smiley when you're around, like when she drinks her favorite coffee."

I can't help but grin at that. "Well, that's good to know. So, you'll help me ask her?"

"Can we ask her now?" Ezra asks, striking a dramatic pose that has me doubled over with laughter.

"How about we let her wake up first?" I ask, pointing to something down the beach. "What's that?"

Ezra races ahead, distracted by the blob that washed up on the shoreline. "Don't touch it," I call. "It could be a jellyfish."

Ezra stops and waits for me. "Is it?" he asks when I catch up.

I nod. "Yep, so we don't want to get too close."

After observing the jellyfish for a while, Ezra insists we turn back and see if Ashlan's awake yet.

"Okay, but we need to discuss the plan first."

❦ ❦ ❦ ❦ ❦

"Mommy," Ezra calls, knocking on her hotel room door. "Time to wake up."

Ashlan answers the door already dressed in a beautiful yellow sundress. "Good morning," she says, bending down to give Ezra a kiss. "I see you've already been down to the beach."

Ezra turns and looks at me, giving me a thumbs up. "Yep, and I want to show you something," he says, grabbing her hand. "Come on."

She laughs. "Hang on, I need to grab my shoes." She slips her feet into a pair of strappy sandals and grabs her room key from the dresser, slipping it into her pocket.

"We need to hurry," Ezra says, pulling her towards the beach entrance.

Her eyebrow quirks up at that, but she smiles and follows his lead. "I'm coming, I'm coming."

As we make our way down to the beach, I feel the weight of the ring box in my pocket. The moment is here. When I shared my plan with Ashlan's mom, she teared up before enthusiastically giving me her blessing. I only hope Ashlan's reaction is just as positive.

"Mom, look!" Ezra points excitedly at the sand.

I let out a relieved sigh when I see the heart with the words "WILL YOU MARRY ME?" in large letters has been left untouched. Ashlan gasps, her hand flying to her mouth as I drop to one knee in front of her and pull out the ring box.

"Ashlan Dewitt," I begin, my voice trembling slightly, "you've brought more joy and love into my life than I ever thought possible. Will you do me the honor of becoming my wife?"

I watch as tears well up in her eyes, a mix of shock and happiness playing across her face. "Oh, Beau," she whispers. "Yes! A thousand times, yes!"

My heart soars. I carefully remove the ring—definitely don't want to have to hire someone to come out with a metal detector to find it in the sand—and slip the diamond onto her finger. Ashlan holds up her hand, smiling at the sight of the new bling displayed there, and pulls me up into a tight embrace. Ezra joins in, wrapping his arms around our legs, his laughter bubbling up between us.

"Group hug!" he shouts, causing us all to laugh.

Just then, a wave comes along and washes away half of my message. "It's a good thing we got here when we did," I say, smiling.

Ashlan giggles. "You didn't need a message in the sand to ask me, I'd have said yes without it."

"Good to know," I say, pulling her close, and cupping her face in my hands. Her green eyes meet mine, full of love and promise. As our lips meet, the world fades away. The kiss is soft and sweet, yet filled with the promise of our future together. When we finally part, I rest my forehead against hers. "I love you, Ashlan Dewitt-soon-to-be-Travers," I murmur.

She smiles that radiant smile that first stole my heart. "And I love you, Beau Travers, my soon-to-be husband."

"Hey, what about me?" Ezra says, jumping up and down beside us.

I lift him into my arms and kiss his cheek. "I love you too, Ezra Dewitt."

"Love you, too, Dad."

*   *   *   *   *

Thank you so much for reading *A Brewtiful Kind of Love*! If you enjoyed the book, I would love it if you'd leave a review. Seeing what readers enjoy about my novels helps me craft better stories! Plus, it puts a huge smile on my face. Want an exclusive map of downtown Piney Brook? Visit https://tinyurl.com/PineyBrookMapfor your FREE bonus content when you join my newsletter.

Looking for more by Tia Marlee? Check out her new series Apple Blossom Ranch, with the first book, *His to Have*, on Amazon and included in Kindle Unlimited. Keep reading for an excerpt from *His to Have*.

Sign up for her newsletter and be the first to find out about upcoming sales, releases and more! www.tiamarlee.com

An Excerpt from His to Have

Book 1 in the Apple Blossom Ranch Series

Patty

Working the morning shift certainly has its perks. Except for the fact I'm not a morning person. I slide my non-skid shoes on and head for the kitchen to grab my steaming mug of coffee. I glance over at my unmade bed and shrug as I take a sip of the nectar of the morning. It can stay unmade. No one's going to be upset about it.

The small studio apartment above the garage of an elderly woman was heaven sent when I rolled into Piney Brook a few months ago.

I fell in love with the small town's charm and decided to stop for a few days. At the time, I'd been thinking I'd go further west, but something about Piney Brook called to me. So, one morning, I stopped into the diner for breakfast and spread out the local paper on the table in front of me circling jobs and rentals that I might be able to get.

When Ms. Daisy saw what I was up to, she offered me a job on the spot. I swear she has a sixth sense about people in need. I took her up on her offer, especially because she didn't mind that I didn't have any experience. "We all start somewhere," she said. By the time I'd finished my first shift, she'd convinced her friend to lease me the studio space above her garage.

A far cry from the stuffy run-down trailer I'd lived in with Klive. I shiver and grab my keys. Getting away from Dixie Pass, Tennessee, and Klive, was the best decision I've ever made.

I step out of the apartment and close the door, locking it securely behind me. Taking the steps two at a time, I make it to the driveway in record time. I might not be late after all.

My light blue Honda Civic, the only possession I'd taken with me when I got married, and the only thing I'd left with, is waiting for me. I pat the hood as I walk by to open the door and slide inside. It's twenty years old, but the ole gal still runs perfectly. Okay, maybe not perfectly, I think as I start it and hear the whine of the belt, I haven't had fixed yet. "Please, Gertie, just a while longer."

I pull out of the parking lot and head toward town. Of course, I get stopped at both red lights between Mrs. Beck's house and Beats and Eats. By the time I park and make it inside to clock in, I'm five minutes late.

I stick my things in the back, and tie on my apron. Time to get busy.

Several hours later, we've made it through the breakfast rush, and most of the lunch rush. I've only got one table, and I'm grateful for the break.

"Order's up," Ricky calls from the kitchen.

I grab a tray and take the plates from the window, situating them so I won't drop them. "Thanks, Ricky," I say, sliding the tray onto one hand and balancing it with the other. I've worked at Beats and Eats for a few months now, and while it's harder than I expected, it's also a lot more fun than I could have imagined. Every day is as different as it is the same.

After the way I lived before . . . let's just say it's a nice change of pace. Though it did take me a few weeks to stop jumping every time Ricky yelled through to the servers. Taking the tray of delicious smelling food, I tread carefully around the corner of the counter and into the dining room.

I stop at the table, balancing the tray on my arm. "A club sandwich, fries, and a side of ranch," I say, handing Gabby, my co-worker, her order. "And a BLT with a side of onion rings." I put Anne's plate in front of her. Making a mental note to call her for an appointment to get my hair done. I'm overdue for a spruce-up, and her salon is the best in town. And not just because it's the only one in town.

"Thanks, Patty," Anne says, dipping an onion ring in Gabby's ranch. "When are you going to let me jazz up your hair?"

I laugh. "I am due for a trim," I say. "Just a trim, though. I'm not ready to go crazy."

She grins and points her half-eaten onion ring in my direction. "One of these days, we are busting you out of your shell."

I hear the bell near the door jingle and glance that way. Ms. Daisy is smiling ear to ear and grabbing menus for the newcomers. "Don't look now," I whisper to the women who have slowly become my friends, "but there's a trio of guys that just walked in that I haven't seen before." I fan myself with my free hand. "I don't think they're from around here." I wink at them both. Gabby's only got eyes for her ex, Heath, but Anne's been talking about finding love. "I'd for sure remember *them*."

Anne chews her bite of food and looks over her shoulder to where I'd motioned. She spins back around, fanning her flushed face. "Oh my," she says, taking a sip of her pop.

"Told ya," I say, bumping my hip against the table before walking away to greet the men now comfortably seated in my station. If only I was as carefree and open to love as Anne. I sigh and clear my throat as I approach the table.

"Hi there, gentlemen. What can I get you to drink?" The three men seated at the table share the same features. Dark brown hair, blue-green eyes, and matching smiles that could blind oncoming traffic. So, brothers, I'm guessing. The one closest to me has little dimple marks on his smoothly shaven cheeks.

Swoon.

I listen as they rattle off their drink order. Sweet teas all around. I grin. "I'll get those right out. My name's Patty, if you need anything."

Dimples winks. "Thanks, sugar." He jerks and leans down to rub his shin. "What was that for?"

The guy sitting across from him smirks. "You can't go around calling people 'sugar.'" He shakes his head. "That's a lawsuit waiting to happen."

I chuckle and shake my head. "'Sugar' is fine with me." I wink. I feel the heat start to bloom in my cheeks. *What's wrong with me?* "Be right back with your drinks," I squeak out. Turning on my heel, I rush to the drink station and start filling cups with ice. My hands are shaking, and I'm debating dunking my face right into the ice bin.

Who winks at a customer?

A very handsome, drool-worthy customer, but still.

I groan. After my divorce from Klein, you'd think I'd have permanent blinders on. I shudder at the thought.

"You gonna make those drinks or wait till the ice melts?" Ms. Daisy's voice startles me and I drop the cup I'm holding, scattering ice everywhere.

"I . . . I'm so sorry, I'll clean that up."

Ms. Daisy laughs. "Just finish making the drinks. I've got the mess." She grabs the broom and dustpan from in the corner and starts sweeping up the spill.

I remake the glass I spilled and add the tea before putting them on a tray and making my way back to the waiting table. "Here we are," I say, carefully placing the drinks on the table. "Sorry about that," I say, sneaking a peek at their left hands. No wedding rings.

"No problem, *sugar*." The man looks pointedly across the table, then turns back to me. "My name's Finn."

I blush. I can feel my cheeks burn with the increased blood flow. Drat having fair skin! "Hello, Finn, and who do you have joining you?" It seems silly to hold introductions, but I appreciate Finn's manners.

"These are two of my brothers, Caleb and Cooper."

I smile at each one in turn. "Nice to meet you. Have y'all decided on what you're having?"

"What would you suggest?" Finn asks. His eyes hold mine a beat longer than necessary.

"I like just about everything here, but you can't go wrong with Ms. Daisy's fried chicken." It's true. I've tried nearly everything on the menu since working here, and it's all delicious, but the fried chicken is next level.

"Great," Finn says, laying the menu on the table. "That's what I'll have."

His brothers chime in, both asking for the same.

"Perfect," I say, tucking my notepad into my apron. "That should be right out."

"Take your time," Caleb says, leaning back in the chair. "I'm in no hurry."

Cooper scoffs and says something I can't quite make out as I walk away. They sure are handsome, and did he say two *of* his brothers? How many men are running around in the world with those genes?

Let's Stay In Touch

You can find me at my website: https://tiamarlee.com
Follow me:
Facebook: https://tinyurl.com/FBTiaMarlee
Instagram: https://tinyurl.com/IGTiaMarlee
Amazon: https://tinyurl.com/AmazonTiaMarlee
BookBub: https://tinyurl.com/BBTiaMarlee
Goodreads: https://tinyurl.com/GRTiaMarlee

Join my reader group: https://tinyurl.com/TiaMarleeReaderGroup

The Coffee Loft

THE COFFEE LOFT IS back with another collection of cozy, stand-alone sweet romcoms—this time served with an extra shot of rugged charm! Wrap yourself in flannel, breathe in the crisp mountain air, and settle in with a new brew. Mountain Brew is bold and smooth, just like the men who drink it. These bearded mountain men may look rough around the edges, but one taste, and they're *irresistibrew!*

Get ready to fall for flawed but lovable heroes, laugh-out-loud dating disasters, mixed signals, surprising twists, and heart-stopping grand gestures guaranteed to make you swoon. Grab your favorite table over in the corner and prepare to be swept off your feet by these unforgettable mountain men.

Find the series here: https://books.bookfunnel.com/thecoffeeloftseriesmountainb...

Guess what else? We have two more series to enjoy. Find them below:

Fall Collection: https://www.amazon.com/dp/B0CXQBFPHK

W   i   n   t   e   r
Collection: https://www.amazon.com/dp/B0CG2MQP2J

Also By Tia Marlee

Piney Brook Wishes Series

His Christmas Wish

Sweet Summertime Wishes

Wishing for the Girl Next Door

A Soldier's Wish

Her New Year's Wish

The Piney Brook Wishes Box Set

The Coffee Loft Series

Bean Wishing for a Latte Love

You Mocha Me Crazy

A Brewtiful Kind of Love

Apple Blossom Ranch Series

His to Have

His to Hold

His to Love
His to Cherish
Hers to Treasure

About the Author

Tia Marlee enjoys delivering swoon worthy HEA's in her clean and wholesome romance novels. A small-town girl at heart, Tia's stories have that small-town, Hallmark charm with a dash of real life, and a laugh thrown in for good measure.

Tia is the author of the Piney Book Wishes series featuring unexpected love stories based in small-town Piney Brook, Arkansas. She is also proud to be part of the multi-author romcom series The Coffee Loft season one and two.

Tia resides in Texas with her husband and three teenaged children. When she's not writing or reading, you can find her standing barefoot in her front yard, loving on her 80-pound lap dog, or hauling kids from one activity to the next.

www.ingramcontent.com/pod-product-compliance
Lightning Source LLC
Chambersburg PA
CBHW051921240626
47153CB00004B/1309